THE NEW FLESH

Keith Deininger

For my loving wife.

Acknowledgements

Special thanks to Amber, whose support for my ambitions, however far-fetched they may be—like publishing a work of fiction—has been unwavering throughout the years; for all those friends who read over my shoulder or listened to my babbling as I worked things out; for Shane Staley, and Dave Thomas, (and Zach McCain, who designed the cover), whose friendly professionalism has impressed me and earned my loyalty; and special thanks to Greg F. Gifune who has shown much enthusiasm for my work and future writing career and who believed in this novel just as I was about ready to give up on it.

PROLOGUE

What Jake's parents didn't know, what they could never understand — what they'd forgotten as they grew older and matured into adulthood — was that the world was a wondrous and mysterious place, and that it was always a matter of perception, that things bubbled and boiled beneath the surface of what could be seen, and felt, and heard; that sometimes these things reached out — like plunging your hand blindly into a murky pool in an attempt to recover a dropped key to the next door before you — and touched you in ways you could never understand.

*   *   *

When he was very little, he used to have these dreams about riding through the open desert on horseback, even though he'd only ever seen such things on the TV and never actually touched a real horse. His dad would tell him stories about their ancestors being some of the first to settle the American Southwest and he'd try real hard to think about what life would have been like back then—sleeping outside, and hunting for food, and gunfights in the streets—but he could never quite figure it out, and soon he started to dream about other things.

Mostly about fire, after what happened—the "incident," his mom called it. He was guilty, and scared. He'd been so mesmerized by the flames he'd lost control.

And sometimes his dreams were vivid, so real he had no way to be sure if he was awake or asleep, or absorbed, perhaps, in a television program. And sometimes he saw things, strange contortions in reality; things that couldn't actually be there, that blossomed from his imagination and hung about as apparitions unnatural to common law, things that were often disturbing in strange ways he could never quite grasp.

Sometimes, in his dreams, he saw the Melting Man.

But his mom and his dad were right: his fantasies weren't real and he believed them. He shouldn't feel guilty for something that had happened over three years ago. He'd stopped having dreams about fire. He'd moved on. His imaginary friend, just as his dad insisted, did not exist.

PART ONE: PARENTS

ONE

It had been his son—whose strangeness, even at the tender age of six—had inspired his most successful screenplay. Never released in mainstream theaters, *The New Flesh* became a cult success as one of the "strangest horror movies of the decade," as quoted from an online e-zine of some repute and plastered on the cover of the DVD release.

But these fucks had never seen it, probably never even heard of it; these fucks could only think in numbers—money churned from the constant production of low-budget pornography and sold to websites such as his—had probably never thought twice about artistic merit or expression before dropping to their knees and licking the shiny leather boots of the Great American Capitalist Machine known affectionately as Uncle "Don't-Call-Me-Motherfucker" Sam.

On the little flat-panel display on the wall of the cramped studio that served as his conference room, Harlan Bowden watched the same old scene — a woman with large fake boobs bent over what was supposed to be her teacher's desk moaning melo-dramatically while a barely in-shape man did her from behind, sucking air through his teeth with every thrust and without much enthusiasm. The men presenting the video, Lee and Derek, one to each side of the table — dressed in "business casual" — wore duplicate, mirthless expressions.

When the video was done — the man blowing his disappointing load across the woman's face and open mouth — the one known as Lee turned to him, folding his hands on the table in front of him: "So..."

Harlan grimaced. "Yeah, I'll buy it. Of course I'll buy the fucking thing. I always do, don't I?"

"Excellent," Lee said, pushing his chair back from the table and already standing.

"Just do one thing for me, will ya?" Harlan asked. "Bring me something new."

Lee, standing now with his briefcase in hand, looked at Harlan blankly.

Derek, still comfortably in his seat, leaned over the table. "What do you mean by *new*, Mr. Bowden?"

"I mean I want something different, exciting; something that pushes the boundaries. I want more than the same five fucking positions. I want story. I want violence. Anything!"

Derek's trimmed eyebrows raised. "Violence, Mr. Bowden?"

"Well, no, not exactly. That's not what I meant. I just want to start a new site; one that's a little more artistic. I have the money; I've been saving. You bring me something that I like, something that really gets my blood pumping, and I'll pay big. You know I will."

"Of course. I'll see what we can do." Derek stood. "Have a good day, Mr. Bowden."

*   *   *

In *The New Flesh*, the little boy Denny watches a lot of television as a way to escape the real world because his parents are always arguing, often violently. He begins to talk to the TV and it is revealed partway through the movie that he is in contact with a being he calls ZigZig—imaginary or otherwise, it is never revealed—who tells Denny about things he could not possibly know. In one scene, Denny sits transfixed before the television set while his parents argue over whether or not they should seek professional psychological help for him in the other room, Denny hearing every word, his face contorted in terror.

*   *   *

The woman's name was Grace and, as usual, she was overdressed for the video shoot. Harlan had asked her once, after another shoot, if she was going to a cocktail party on Mulholland Drive later, but she'd only shrugged, given him her sarcastic smile, and said: "You only live once. I just want to look good while I still look good."

Sitting in a couple of folding chairs, they watched

the procession together, as they had numerous times before. Other producers sat in a tight little semi-circle with them. It was hot, humid; the sweat was in the air they breathed, the smells sour and organic. Harlan sighed inwardly, glanced at the others—pressed denim jeans and greasy light-colored shirts unbuttoned around the throat for the men, the woman also in jeans with flats on their feet and hair pulled back and up in messy swirls—sitting in their little chairs like lazy directors, some nodding slightly, others only watching intently through the curls of cigarette smoke. Serious faces—seeing money in each hump, in each moan; seeing the stenciled-green faces of dead presidents printed across each breast and butt cheek, along the shaft of each penis. He shifted in his chair, rubbed his temples absently against the looming headache. The director was telling one of the women to lie on her back while the other woman straddled her in the classic "69" position. He directed the man to stand behind the redhead. How creative, Harlan thought sarcastically, pressing his fingers along his temples.

After the shoot, people mingled, as they always did, discussing the new video and the industry. Harlan brooded in a corner, a Crown and Coke sweating in his hand. The drinks seemed to be helping his headache a little and people seemed to sense he was in no mood for casual discussion and were, for the most part, letting him be. He couldn't wait for this tiresome obligation to be over so he could get back to his apartment, draw the shades, maybe have a few more drinks, and pass out on the couch watching an old classic from his movie collection—his *regular* movie collection.

Grace, her flowing, vibrant dress unmistakably red amongst the shouldered earth tones, was walking up to him. *Oh great, here we go,* Harlan thought.

"Enjoying the party?" she asked, her lips already showing signs of her sardonic smirk.

Harlan huffed. "Yeah, right. Party? This thing?"

Grace leaned casually against the wall next to him. "Actually," she said, "I know what you mean. I've been coming to these things for a while now and nothing much has changed over the years. I'm just so sick of all...this." She waved her open hand at the mumbling crowd. "I've grown bored of the whole charade." She shrugged. "But what else is there? Maybe I'll retire soon. Who knows?"

Harlan nodded absently, knowing it was all just small talk, expecting her to go on, perhaps asking him his opinion on the evening's shoot, but she didn't.

After a while, she said, "I wish someone would bring us something new and exciting. There's simply no creativity in our industry, I'm afraid."

Harlan looked at the woman, noticing for the first time the fullness of her lips, her pale cheeks flushed lightly from the martinis she was drinking. "I've been feeling the same way."

Grace turned to face him fully, the alcohol and the noise from the room drawing them close. "I thought that might be the case," she breathed. "I could tell by the way you were sitting there watching the shoot."

Harlan's head buzzed. "I've been looking for something..." he began, "something new. I used to be a screenwriter, you know." He must be getting drunk if he was sharing things like this with her.

"Really? I used to be an actress," she said, "and not in pornography—a real actress; television mostly, a few commercials, but movies too."

Harlan nodded. "I could have guessed that."

Grace blushed, clearly pleased with the remark. "What do you say we escape this sleazy little hell-hole?" she said, proffering her arm.

Harlan circled his arm over hers. "Why not?"

Grace smiled, slightly canted. "Shall we?"

*   *   *

There was a small package—wrapped in brown paper, not in his mail slot, but leaned upright against the foot of the door to his apartment—waiting for him. Harlan bent, snatched it up, tucked it beneath his arm and fumbled the keys from his pocket. Grace stood patiently behind him, leaning on one leg so that her hip curved to one side dramatically.

Harlan dropped the package by the door and left Grace to putter about the living room while he made drinks in the kitchen.

"Is this your kid?" Grace called out across the apartment.

"Yeah, you must have found a picture of Jake. That's my son."

"Adorable."

"He's a weirdo."

Grace laughed.

When Harlan entered the living room with their drinks, Grace was standing in front of the couch holding the brown paper package, turning it from side to side. "It feels like a CD case," she said, a slight crease running between her eyes.

Harland took the package from her and handed Grace her martini. He tossed the package on the end table, sipped his drink.

Grace was looking at him. "Well? Aren't you going to open it?"

"Later."

"Oh come now, I'm not here to pry. Aren't you curious? No name; no return address—what could it be?"

"Alright. Fine. Let's see what it is."

Harlan set his drink down and took up the package. He ripped the paper away and tossed it by his feet. He turned the CD jewel case in his hands; it was blank, no labels. Grace was by his shoulder, "Oh, what is it?" He flipped the case open to a blank DVD, one of those cheap ones you can buy in the spindle.

Harlan shrugged. "Let's try it." He stood, took a couple of steps across the room to his entertainment center, opened the extravagant doors with row after row of DVDs meticulously categorized, to his 90" LCD flat screen, and slid the blank disc into the player. He dropped back into the couch next to Grace and flicked the screen to life with the remote.

"Impressive collection. What are all those?"

Harlan powered on the DVD player and hit PLAY on the remote. "Horror movies mostly, but there are other things too."

Grace nodded.

The screen flickered in the dimly lit apartment. A room came into view, framed in medium shot—a small room, tiled floors, a grand red curtain pulled across the background, and a single piece of furniture; a table made from three large slabs of stone, the largest resting atop the other two.

Grace leaned forward eagerly.

Harlan lit a cigarette.

For a minute or two, it was only the room. Then, a woman in panties and bra stepped into the scene, tiptoed like the room was cold, and climbed up onto the stone table. She looked at the camera, blinked a couple of times. A man came after her; he was wearing a mask of large, dark pooled eyes and an exuberant cartoon grin. He held a dangling coil of chain in one hand. Another man followed the first, this one wearing an equally hideous mask, its stretched mouth turned down to a droopy frown. The two men used the chain, wrapping it beneath the table and over, tying the woman in place about her waist.

"What is this?" Grace breathed.

"I don't know."

Both men, the happy and the sad one, produced black leather whips from the folds of their robes and began taking turns whipping the restrained woman. The woman cried out with each lash.

Grace shifted in her seat. "Is this real?"

"I don't think so," Harlan said.

What followed was a not-entirely-original torture and sex scene. The men took turns, one holding the woman down while the other fucked her furiously. There was slapping and roughness. At one point, the woman bit the happy-masked man, who yelped in surprise. But mostly it was a brutal scene that ended with both men bent over the writhing woman, choking her until she was still.

When the video stopped, there was stillness in

the apartment, the air buzzed with silence.

Slowly, Harlan bent and picked the discarded wrapping paper from the ground, turning it, looking for a clue as to who might have sent him this video. Is this what they thought he was looking for? He broke the silence: "That was a little weird, huh?"

"Yeah."

He turned to look at Grace for the first time since the video had started—her bosom was heaving, her eyes smoldering, pupils dilated.

She licked her swollen lips. "Kiss me," she said.

*   *   *

"ZigZig told me about other worlds. One's in there," Denny says in Harlan's only produced film outside of the porn industry.

Denny's father: "In where?"

"There," Denny says, pointing at the TV screen jagged with snow, his face soft with wonder.

"What's it like in there?"

"Lightning and fire." A whisper: "Lightning and fire."

TWO

Last night, Jake had had that nightmare again—the familiar one, the one he hadn't dreamt in a while, the one where he didn't put the fire out, where he couldn't put it out, and flickering orange flames spread and burned, lurching around in their creepy dance. It had been bad this time; bad enough to stay with him while he sat at the kitchen table trying to choke down his bowl of fast-going-soggy Lucky Charms; bad enough that he jumped when his mom cleared her throat behind him, shuffling past in her droopy coffee-stained robe; bad enough he couldn't help himself from staring at the little orange spot of flame at the end of the match as his mother moved it to the tip of her cigarette.

"Do I have to go to school today, Mom?"

"Of course. It's only Tuesday. Why? Are you not feeling good?" She picked up her muffin, put it back down, took hold of her mug (pictures of cartoon cats cavorting around its rim), and sipped her coffee.

"I'm not sick or anything. I just—" Jake tried to think what he could say, how he could get his mom to understand how he felt. "I don't know," he said, sighing into the bowl of grayish-blue milk leftover from his cereal. "I guess I'll just go to school."

"Good. Now hurry up and get dressed. You're going to be late."

Jake shuffled down the hallway to his room.

There was a bus that could take him, but he only lived a couple miles from school, so he usually walked. Besides, the bus was too crowded, too noisy, too many kids screaming and throwing things. It made him uncomfortable—his face would flush, his palms would sweat—he didn't fit in. He didn't like being squished against the cold thin steel of the bus's frame, his breath fogging the window, his butt sticking on the plastic seat, the kid next to him who wouldn't sit still, bouncing, jigging; yelling to be heard over all the other kids. He preferred to walk; it was only a couple of miles and he liked being outdoors. Sometimes his friend Jesse, who lived a couple of blocks down the street, would walk with him, or Jesse's mom would give them a ride, but most of the time he walked alone.

Today, the morning air was crisp and cool. Before long, he forgot about the nightmare and his earlier trepidations. He moved easy, whistling softly to himself (a talent he'd practiced for countless hours in his room to master and was quite proud of). His walk took him through the neighborhood. He passed Jesse's house and came up to Old Man Greene's perfectly green and meticulously manicured lawn. Greene's house was a corner lot and Greene was known to chase kids that dared to cut across his lawn on their way to and from school away with a broom; Jake was careful to use the sidewalk. He passed Johnny's place, known to most of the kids Jake's age as 'Johnny the Babysitter' because he picked up extra cash watching kids around the neighborhood and let you watch rated R movies if you wanted to. Then he came upon Mrs. Marlow's extravagantly gardened yard and her collection of plastic gnomes spread throughout the lush vegetation.

When he reached the construction zone, where the suburb came to a halt, he cut across the street. Since the company that had been working on the housing expansion project had suddenly gone bankrupt a couple of years ago, several of the plots had been cleared and now stood empty and abandoned, leaving, in some places, the skeletal husks of houses that would probably never be built.

On the other side of the street was a large apartment complex. Cutting through a pathway between the uninspiring brown buildings with their highspire roofs, he came upon a dirt bike path skirting the edge of the creek that ran through the middle of the neighborhood. The creek wasn't really a creek, but more of a ditch for water runoff, to keep the neighborhood from flooding, a flat expanse of sand cut through with shallow rivulets of water. He often spent time wandering the creek and playing in the water, and sometimes, when he had more time, walked to school along the sandy bed itself. Today, however, he took the path, walking briskly, passing over the large concrete, algae-encrusted drainage pipe that was like an opening into the caverns beneath the city, passing the swampy area with the tadpoles and the little frogs you could catch, and out into the playground at the back of his school. A little ways farther along, there was a small, forested area the locals called Sherwood Forest where Jake had built his tree house. Three years ago, he'd started the fire in there, started the fire he couldn't put out—a charred area of black, still barren of all growth even after two years, as if some kind of demon had risen there, coming up from beneath the earth, blighting that spot, marking it for future entrance.

School, that day, was boring—as usual.

* * *

Fire — he'd learned once he'd really seen it in action — lives and dies by its own sordid rules. It hypnotizes: so small, then multiplying. Its flickers don't appear real, but it heats the cheeks and the bridge of the nose, sitting crouched before a pile of leaves, a pack of matches in his grubby hands. It mesmerizes, erases the rational mind. It is primal and it is powerful. It dances and it eats, and grows and looks for more.

And it's everywhere and he is afraid he started it; he must have started it. He falls into these trances and he just can't help himself. He licks his lips and lights the matches and he hardly knows what he's doing. He lights the dried leaves like insect crusts and he stares at the little flames licking up their sides and folding over and upwards and when he has a chance to stop things from getting out of control — to stomp out the flames under the rubber soles of his Keds – he just watches and feels the tingling heat on his face and hands. It's just, he's not in control of himself; he feels good in these moments; it feels only natural to let go of himself and bask in the hunger of the flames. Let it burn, he sometimes thinks, as he inhales the acrid smoke.

Then everything is burning. In the forest grove, the branches of the trees above enshroud the scene in lowly crackling flame; the bushes sputter and crunch like the carcasses of dead animals, brittle bones snapping one then another; the underbrush sizzles, smoke rising from the tender green foliage going gray, losing color. He looks up and out between the burning branches and the horizon is black and he can see his school and the playground is burning and there are horses in a panic in the soccer field, whinnying and kicking the smoke-filled air with their hooves – the monkey bars melted and sagging – and the buildings are charred behemoths.

"It's beautiful, don't you think?"

The voice is right over his shoulder, but he doesn't want to turn; he can feel the cool spray of breath on the back of his neck.

"But it's about more than esthetics. It shows us what life is really about, wouldn't you agree? It eats and eats for as long as it can, as much as it can, and then dies and only the charred remnants of its destruction are left behind."

He shudders. "I..." he begins, "I want to wake up now."

The voice inhales like water droplets hitting a fry pan. "Of course, but don't worry. All you have to do is remember; you must not forget: you can change the world and I can help you."

"But..."

"Not now. You can go. It's okay."

He begins to turn. Oh God. He doesn't want to turn. He can feel his heart pounding at his ribcage. He can feel his hands sweaty and trembling. If he turns, he'll see that face; he doesn't want to see that face. But he can't help it. This is what happens at the end of the dream; this is what always happens.

But the face is already fading back into the flaming foliage. He only catches a glimpse – a face like melting grease, flesh running and pooling about a wide grin of shark's teeth; pointed ears bent, striated with pulsing veins; eyes looking out through the shifting miasma bright and mischievous. And he tries to look away, to force himself to awaken from the nightmare like pulling himself from a warm drowning pool. He struggles, but his body will not move.

"Someday," the voice of the Melting Man, high and crisp, says, already fading, muffled as if speaking from the other side of a window, "you'll have to follow me and see what happens. I can show you things. Beautiful things. You'll see."

The boy gapes. He can feel himself shaking all over. His heart beats frantically at his chest like a cornered animal.

Wake up! Wake up! Wake up!

The face of the Melting Man continues to fade backwards, then bulges, inflating from the side so that one eye expands – the quivering glare of a runny egg – and there is a gleeful tittering like a cruel cartoon or fun-house clown taking pleasure in repulsing its young audience.

Wake up! Please! Wake up!

*   *   *

Someone was shaking him. He opened his eyes. Jesse loomed over him.

"Wake up. Come on. Recess is over, Jake. It's time for Social Studies."

"Uh, hey."

"What the hell, Jake? Falling asleep on the soccer field? You're a weirdo."

Jake smiled ruefully, his dream already a distant memory. "Yeah, that's what my dad says."

THREE

In college, she'd had a choice. Unfortunately, with what she believed were her best years behind her, it seemed she'd made the wrong one.

Jessica pulled open one of the kitchen drawers; it was filled with various random household supplies: a pair of scissors, an old pocket knife, a roll of tape, unopened envelopes of mail (mostly billing statements), markers and pens, a tangle of headphones and USB cords, and — shoved towards the back — her last two mini bottles of vodka. She grasped both bottles in the fingers of one hand and set them on the counter.

Jessica looked at the bottles and sighed. In the morning she could go and get more, but, for tonight, these were her last.

A gust of wind rattled a tree branch against the dark glass of the kitchen window.

Without further hesitation, she picked up one of the bottles, twisted off its tiny red cap, and upended its contents down her throat: *gurgle-slurp, gurgle-slurp, gurgle-slurp.* She gulped; grimaced; waited, feeling the warmth spread in her chest, and then tossed the bottle into the trashcan by the side of the counter.

Jake was upstairs, sleeping. *He's a good kid,* Jessica thought. *Thank God for that.*

In college, she hadn't dated much, only gone out with two different men. One, her now ex-husband Harlan, had been her first. Harlan had been sweet and charming back then, a little shy, with a dark and passionate artistic side he shared only with those closest to him, guarding his writing and his pad of pencil sketches with a fierce self-consciousness.

A couple of weeks into their relationship, he'd climbed through the window into her dorm room while she was away and spread and hid little scraps of paper torn from one of his lined school notebooks in every nook and cranny. When she'd returned from class she found them. *I love the way your nose wrinkles when you laugh,* one of the notes said. *You're cute,* said another. *You have a great smile.* And one of them said, simply: *Sexy haircut.* In those days Harlan hadn't had money for flowers or chocolates, but he'd still managed to flatter and impress her in all the right ways.

She'd kept all those note scraps in a plastic pencil box collected with a few pictures from her first couple of semesters, but, somewhere over the years, she'd lost the box and everything in it.

One time, at a party maybe six months into their relationship, Harlan had left her standing up against the side of the house smoking a cigarette, and staggered over to a couple of guys from the college rugby team wearing lettermen jackets, like they were still in high school.

"You guys are total fucking douche bags, you know that?" he'd said.

The muscle-heads stared down at Harlan. "Fuck off. Get out of here," one of them said.

Harlan took a pull from the bottle of cheap rum he held at his side. "The truth is," he began, "ninety-nine percent of the people you'll meet in this lifetime are completely worthless pieces of shit and will never have anything of any value to contribute to the world."

The muscle-heads continued to stare, looking unsure whether they should be insulted.

"Like you guys," Harlan continued. He raised his hands and shook them around mockingly, the rum sloshing noisily in its bottle. "You think you're so strong; you can sleep with lots of girls. Like that means anything. You're not better than anyone else. You're stupid, worthless pieces of shit. You're like this scrap of gum on the bottom of my shoe." Harlan raised one of his feet and pointed with his free hand, then stumbled and put his foot back down.

One of the rugby players stepped forward, but the other put his hand out to stop him. The rugby player sneered and shook his head. "This guy's not worth it," and turned and spat into the dirt.

"You're right," Harlan said, and threw the muscle heads a wicked smirk. "I'm no better than you guys. I'm a stupid, worthless piece of shit too."

And with that Harlan had cackled, turned, and sauntered back to where Jessica still stood against the house watching. He'd come right up to her, thrown his arm around her waist, and pulled her into an impassioned and sloppy kiss.

She'd taken him by the hand, then, and led him back into the house, through the groups of milling partiers, and into the bathroom, where she went down on him, sucking him off until he came, swallowing what he had to give her.

Harlan had been exciting, quick-witted when he wanted to be, and a lot of fun to be around. It was years before she even thought twice about the pills he took and how they might have something to do with his mood swings.

And, sometimes, they had fights: grand dramatic performances of yelling and screaming and blaming and cursing, over things she rarely remembered afterwards. Harlan had pitiful moments of self-loathing where he'd begin to insult their relationship under his breath. She ignored these insults as long as possible, but when she could no longer stand it, she'd confront him and the fighting would begin.

It was during one of these breakups that she met Trevor, the other guy she dated in college.

One afternoon, she'd been studying alone at a table in the Student Union Building—more concerned with her recent breakup than with the chapter she was going over on the "stigma of psychological disorders"—when this guy with messy dark hair and a worn leather jacket had approached her.

"Are you okay?"

Jessica looked up to tell this stranger she was fine and would he please leave her alone, but she took one look into those eyes—dark saucers with almost no color, clear and intelligent — and the words caught in her throat, her annoyance forgotten.

"Are you sure you're okay?" he repeated.

She crossed her arms over her chest. "Fine."

He sat down across the table from her. "My name is Trevor. And yours is…Jess. Am I right?"

She looked at him closely. Only her friends called her Jess. She nodded noncommittally. "How did you know that?"

"I don't know. I must have heard it somewhere."

"Look — "

"Would you like to go out?"

"What?"

"Dinner: would you have it with me?"

Jessica wrinkled her nose. "Really? Just like that?"

Trevor shrugged. "Why not?"

There was something compelling about him, something dangerous. "I don't think so," she said.

"Okay." He stood and walked away.

She watched him leave. "That was strange," she mumbled to herself.

But after that brief encounter, she hadn't been able to get him out of her head. She began to have dreams about him and caught herself sometimes playing out their brief encounter differently, imagining how it would have gone if she'd said yes; how he would have smiled and asked if she liked lobster, which, of course, she did. She imagined getting lost in those dark eyes, while he held her; confident he'd never let her fall; never let her go.

A couple of days after the encounter, she'd been scrambling some eggs in the shared kitchen in her dorm. It was a cloudy morning and a pall of gray

seemed to tint the grass and the concrete walk outside, and the students, pale and etherized, floated
grudgingly on their way to class. She wiped the
crust from the corners of her eyes with the back of
her spatula-wielding hand and a movement caught
her attention; she looked out the little kitchen window and he was there, standing by a park bench on
the other side of the courtyard, grinning at her. He
waved once, then turned and walked away down the
sidewalk.

Later, she was at dinner with him and he was telling her a story about a date he'd been on once and
she was laughing. "This girl, at one point during the
meal, actually looked at me, in all seriousness, and
said: 'Ketchup is what makes Americans fat.' Isn't
that a weird thing to hear on a first date? But what
made it so hilarious at the time was that she was actually dipping her fries in her ketchup while she said
it, this distant awe-struck look on her face. It was so
weird I had to stifle a snort of laughter and I bumped
the table and her glass of Merlot splashed the front
of her dress and her, uh, considerable bosom, was
zipped up so tight that, I kid you not, the wine actually pooled in her cleavage and all I could think was:
'Okay, but who's going to drink it now?' I couldn't
help myself after that. I burst into laughter and I was
still laughing when my date stood and stormed out
of the restaurant." Jess laughed at his story, and she
felt comfortable and safe with him, and he laughed
too, and when she looked up from her plate of lobster
tails, his eyes were huge and dark and too big for his
head and that's when she awoke with a start, panting
in the darkness of her dorm room, sweat beading on

her forehead.

Days later, he'd tapped her on the shoulder while she waited in line at one of the restaurants for a quick lunch in the Student Union Building and, when she turned and saw it was him, her heart fluttered in her chest like a cornered bird.

He smiled—a kind, normal smile—and she immediately felt at ease.

"Hello, Jess. How are you?" he said, still smiling.

"I'm good."

"Are you? Excellent. How about going out with me?"

She looked into his eyes and something inside her jittered excitedly. "Where would you take me?"

"Well, I was thinking, some place normal." He was cool and confident. "Pizza? How does that sound?"

Before she could think to stop herself, it slipped out: "Okay."

"Fantastic! We'll go see a movie afterwards; anything, your choice."

She had gone out with Trevor for the next six months. It all seemed surreal now when she thought back on it. Trevor was smooth and serious and Jessica enjoyed spending time with him, but she'd never really loved him. She liked everything he did—his confident and straightforward attitude; his opening doors for her; his expensive gifts of flowers and jewelry—but she never felt the same warmth with Trevor that she felt with Harlan. Trevor was courteous and charming, but he didn't understand her like Harlan did and he made her feel uneasy sometimes, something she couldn't explain.

It was inevitable then, that when Harlan came to win her back, she was forced to dump Trevor and get back together with her first love.

That was the only time she'd seen Trevor lose his cool. He'd been scary then, but she couldn't really blame him. After that, he'd disappeared and her life with Harlan had begun.

But now, looking back on things, she couldn't help but wonder what her life would have been like with Trevor. Harlan had been so full of life, spontaneous and energetic, but he'd been unstable; and Harlan had lost himself when his writing career failed; he'd fallen heavily into his opiate addiction; he'd given up and sold out to the porn industry and a part of him had died. There was no other way she could think to put it.

Now, with the ink on her divorce papers still fresh and her looks beginning to fail her (she hated the lines that deepened around her eyes when she smiled), it was hard not be nostalgic; it was hard not to think of Trevor's dark and compelling gaze; his strong arms holding her, squeezing her tight.

Jessica sighed and looked at the last mini bottle of vodka, sitting lonesome on the kitchen counter. She snatched it, ripped the cap off, and downed it in two burning gulps. She tossed the bottle into the trashcan and turned to leave the kitchen.

There was a knock at the door.

She froze, suddenly aware of the howling wind and the darkness just outside. Who could it be at this time of night?

She shuffled to the front door and looked through the peephole, but it was too dark to see anything—

the porch light bulb had burnt out weeks ago and she still hadn't replaced it (Harlan had always been the one to replace the bulbs when they went dead).

"Who's there?" she called out, scolding herself for the slight waver she heard in her voice.

No answer.

She slid the chain from its runner, turned the bolt, and opened the door slowly, just a crack, peering through the gap.

She let the door swing slowly open, her mouth gaping, her arms falling limp by her sides.

Trevor was standing on the front porch, grinning at her, his leather jacket zipped up against the cold wind, an extravagant bouquet of flowers held out to her.

"Hello, Jess. How are you? Do you think I could come in?"

FOUR

Harlan pulled Grace's arm towards him to get a better look, examining the red and puffy rub-burn marks scored across her wrists and the scrapes along the delicate paleness under her forearms. He made a face and she jerked her arm away, rolling over in the bed to face away from him, the bed sheets pulling tight over her curves.

Harlan shook a cigarette from his pack on the nightstand. "We should stop this," he said, the cigarette jutting wildly from his mouth. "This is just crazy. I really hurt you this time—I know I did. It's just…it's too much."

Grace rolled onto her back, careful to tuck the sheets over the swell of her breasts. "Do you mind?" she said, lifting her hand out for a cigarette.

Harlan shook another from the pack and passed it to her. "It's just; it gets a little crazier every time.

It feels like I'm losing control. I'm not normally like this."

Grace cleared her throat. "Light?"

Harlan grabbed the lighter from the nightstand and lit Grace's cigarette, then his own.

"It's like...I don't know...like there's someone else inside me, someone vicious who...you know... enjoys it."

Grace smiled. "Darling," she said. "Stop this. It's not attractive. I'm fine."

"How long have we been seeing each other?"

Grace shrugged. "A week?"

Harlan dragged deeply on his cigarette, talking through the exhaled smoke. "Christ! It feels like so much longer, don't you think? And every night it gets worse. We need to...I don't know...take a break or something."

Grace shook her head. "No. Harlan honey, it's okay. Please don't worry about it."

Harlan, frustrated at Grace's cool nonchalance, snatched suddenly at the sheets and flung them down the bed.

Grace covered herself instinctively, but Harlan could still see the marks his teeth had made across her breasts, jagged crescents already beginning to bloom purple. "See! Look! I did that! I hurt you! You're already bruising!"

Grace sat up suddenly, her face bristling, dropping her hands to her sides, allowing the fullness of her bosom to show. "Harlan," she said, "shut the fuck up. If I didn't like it, do you think I'd still be here? So shut it. I don't want to talk about it anymore. Shut your fucking mouth!"

Harlan slumped.

Grace grabbed the sheets and pulled them up to her shoulders. She turned away from him. "Jesus Christ," she breathed.

Harlan's heart was racing. This was the first time he'd seen Grace lose her cool, at least like this. He crushed his cigarette out in the ashtray and stood, slowly, carefully. He crept out of the room, leaving Grace alone in his bedroom to cool off.

He made his way to the kitchen. The late-morning sun cut through the blinds over the window, slicing the air into segments of swirling dust and dander. He poured scotch into a mug, gulped down a burning swallow. He'd never been with someone quite like Grace—that cool, go-to-hell attitude that melted into the naughty school girl in the bedroom, begging for his abuse, demanding his bites, teasing his animal impulses to the surface with the cocky way she crossed and uncrossed her legs, the way she glanced over the smoothness of her shoulder, eyes smoldering, lips swollen, mouth slightly open so that the tiny white tips of her teeth showed.

Harlan gulped the rest of what was in his mug, splashed a little more from the bottle. He opened the fridge and started stacking things on the counter. He thought he'd make breakfast—eggs and toast with jam—and then check in on Grace. Then, later, maybe he'd go into the office and make sure things were still running smoothly. He hadn't done more than speak to his lead web designer Wesley Hindeman a few times over the phone, and, since he was usually more hands-on with his business, thought a week's vacation was long enough.

Something thumped at the door.

Harlan froze with an egg in his hand, hovering over the rim of a bowl, and waited for the second knock, which was a habit of his. When none came, he set the egg down in a groove in the kitchen counter and went to the door, opening it and peeking outside. He looked down the apartment hallway—there was no one there. At his feet, however, was a small package wrapped in plain brown paper with no label. He scooped it up and closed the door.

It was another DVD, he could tell, even as he ripped the paper away—same as before: an unlabeled disc.

"Grace," he called, falling into the couch. "You might want to come out here."

"What?" Grace said with annoyance in her voice, walking into the living room. She was in her pink rayon robe, the one from the small suitcase she'd brought over from her place.

"We got another one."

Her annoyed tone dropped instantly, replaced with a restrained excitement. "Oh, really? Did you see who left it this time?"

"No, but I think it's those scumbags, Lee and Derek."

"You do?"

"Yeah, I mentioned something to them a couple of weeks ago about wanting something new and different." Harlan shrugged. "It must be them."

Grace took a seat by Harlan on the couch. "Let's watch it," she said.

"Yeah, alright," Harlan said, flipping open his entertainment center. He felt his heart sputter with excitement. Harlan wasn't really in to this violent stuff, but the first video had been such a turn on for Grace they'd viewed it several times, even fucked with it on in the background.

Harlan pulled the blinds closed and the living room filled with a phosphorescent blue glow before the video started.

Like before, the initial medium shot showed the room with the stone table at its center and the crimson theater curtain serving as a backdrop. A couple of minutes went by without change.

"Did you see the curtain move?" Grace asked.

Harlan looked more closely. "I think it's just an optical illusion. I don't see anything."

Then the man in the frowning drama mask entered, carrying a bundle of chains like in the first video. He shuffled to one side of the stone table and looked directly at the camera, his eyes shadowed beneath the ridges of the mask. The man in the other mask, the smiling one, followed shortly, pulling a naked woman along behind him by a leash. The woman struggled, but only halfheartedly; she took a seat on the stone table. For a moment, both men stopped what they were doing and, turning their heads slowly, stared into the camera, happy and sad faces, placid and serious, as if they could see—like voyeurs through a window—into the living room of Harlan's apartment, watching for the reactions of the man and woman who sat on the couch there, staring back with naked excitement, and perhaps the slightest of trepidations.

The scene that followed was similar to the first: an amateur sex scene followed by the choking of the woman, supposedly to death. Having been in the pornography business for years, Harlan could tell how staged it all was.

Partway through the video, Grace mentioned she might know the girl on the stone table from somewhere. "Yes," she said, "I know her. I used to work with her."

"Yeah?"

"Yeah. That's her."

When the video ended, fading to black, Harlan meant to ask Grace more about the woman from the video, but when he turned she was already touching herself, writhing upon the spilled pink tangle of her robe, her bare flesh glistening in the dim lighting.

"Please," she said. "Hurt me."

*   *   *

"I think I might be able to find the people who made it."

"Uh-huh."

"What was her name? Karen? Caroline? Something normal like that. Even when I knew her years ago she was already involved with these guys who liked to make violent films."

Harlan hunched at the edge of the bed turning his hands over, staring at them as if they weren't his; they were trembling visibly.

"They had a studio somewhere here in town. I think it was downtown; one of those shitty warehouse setups. One of those horrible, drafty places that's always chilly and a little creepy at night."

Harlan looked up at Grace, sitting up in his bed,

as she talked — her eyes bright and alive, her crimson lips teased into a slight smirk. His eyes dropped to her neck and the ring of purple bruises beginning to flower there.

"Yes," Grace was saying, "if I make a few calls I'm sure I can track them down. Oh yes, darling, I'm sure I can find them."

"Did I hurt you?" Harlan interrupted.

Grace met his gaze. "Harlan, honey, I'm fine."

"You don't look fine," he said, nodding to the bruises on her neck.

Grace laughed. "Auto-erotic asphyxiation I believe it's called. Very intense. Although I'll admit, for a moment there, I almost thought you weren't going to let go this time."

"Yeah."

"Tomorrow I'll find out who's making and sending you these videos. Isn't this exciting, Harlan?"

The last twenty minutes was a blank spot in his mind.

"Yeah," Harlan said.

FIVE

"Whoa, Dad, what's this?" Jake held a red bra up by the strap so that it dangled in front of him.

"Where did you get that?" Harlan said, and tried to snatch it from Jake, who pulled it just out of reach.

"I found it in the couch. Is it Mom's?"

"What? No, it's not your mother's. You know better than that." Harlan lunged again, but Jake stood up on the couch, balling the garment against his side so his dad couldn't grab it.

Jake dropped into the couch, tucking the garment beneath him; his dad attacked with his hands, tickling the soft exposed spots beneath Jake's arms until he was kicking and squealing. "Give it to me," his dad growled. "Give me the bra, Jake."

"No. I won't. It's mine—"

"Come on, Jake. Give it to me."

Jake pushed himself as deep into the couch as he could. He giggled helplessly. His dad began to shake him, playfully at first. He dug even farther into the couch and held on. But, when his dad's shaking started to get rougher and rougher, he knew he shouldn't push it.

"Okay…okay…okay," he gave in, holding the bra up.

His dad pulled it from his fingers, twisting them painfully. "Ow," Jake said, shaking his hand.

His dad stormed down the hall with the bra. There was a commercial on the TV for car insurance—ruffian horsemen riding after a car with clubs and spears—muffled sounds; blinking colors in the dim lighting. He sat on the couch and waited until his dad came back.

He heard his dad sigh loudly from across the living room; his dad came and sat down next to him. "Are you okay, Jake?"

"Yeah, I'm fine," and a snort of laughter escaped him.

His dad turned to him and he was smiling. "Are you sure? You're making some strange noises there. Kinda looks like there might be something wrong with you."

Jake tried to look serious. "No. Nope. Nothing."

"Really? You sure about that?"

Harlan attacked Jake with renewed energy, tickling and tickling, until Jake was screaming with laughter, writhing about on the couch, kicking his feet uncontrollably.

When his dad finally stopped, Jake looked up and saw his dad was laughing now too, panting a little, with sweat on his brow. Jake grinned and his dad grinned back. It was nice to get to hang out with his dad once in a while, Jake thought. It was nice to roughhouse without mom looming over them, telling them to quit it.

It was also nice to see his dad smiling. They'd spent the afternoon playing cards, which was unusual. He spent most of his weekends — he lived with his dad on Saturday and Sunday, with his mom the rest of the week — on the Xbox or watching movies from his dad's collection (except for a few that were forbidden), while his dad was in the other room with his computer or pacing about the house on the phone, talking in an endless stream, losing his temper and yelling. This weekend his dad hadn't been distracted by his work, hadn't seemed concerned with it, and he'd been in a good mood for once.

"Hey," his dad said, "what do you want for dinner tonight? I could make something. Or we could just order a pizza again; what do you think?"

"Pizza's good."

"Alright, pizza it is."

*　　*　　*

The cardboard pizza box sat open on the coffee table; grease stains like the shapes of countries on a map; gnawed-on half-moon crusts discarded like bones in a clumsy heap. His dad was in the other room (working), and he was left alone, trying to read a Roald Dahl book, but unable to concentrate.

After a while, he put the book down and went to look through his dad's movie collection for the billionth time. He scanned the rows of DVDs listlessly; his dad really liked horror movies; Jake didn't care for them much himself. He still had nightmares over those little girls in "The Shining" from that time he'd watched it with his dad a year ago.

He chose one of the Indiana Jones movies; it didn't matter which one; he'd seen them all over and over again, even the new one, which his dad said "sucked big-time" compared to the original films. He pried open the plastic case and pulled the disc out; he opened the DVD player.

There was a DVD already in the tray; it was blank: unlabeled.

I wonder what's on this one, Jake thought. He shrugged, and flicked the button, watching the DVD player slide closed over the disc. He was curious.

*   *   *

Harlan closed all the windows on his computer and stared at the image he had set as his wallpaper: a family picture, taken on a hiking trip some weekend a couple of years ago; little Jake's eyes were bugged from his perch upon Jess's shoulders, one arm up-raised, brandishing a stick he'd picked up along the way; a moment of joy — unencumbered, in that single frame — by his parent's emotional turmoil. Jess looked happy too: in her hiking clothes, a slight smirk, rolling her eyes knowingly at Harlan while she tried to keep her balance and give a piggyback ride to their bouncing son.

Harlan missed his family, the way it used to be — the closeness and the laughter. He missed how it was after he'd sold his screenplay: the new house and the brand-new-off-the-lot Subaru; the weekends out skiing and spa trips to Vegas; reading to Jake at night and the serious looks his son would give him at certain moments in the stories he read, Jake's face screwing up, asking, "Why doesn't the wolf just buy a steamroller and roll over the little pigs' houses?"

Then, after Jake had fallen asleep, Jess from the doorway in her nightgown whispering: "You're a good father, you know that?"

"Oh yeah? What do fathers get when they're good?"

Cocking her head to the side, "Oh, I don't know." Then she'd saunter down the hallway to their bedroom swinging her hips — her "sexy" walk — and he'd stifle a laugh, and so would she, and then they would make love as quietly as they could.

But the money hadn't lasted long. He'd tried to write something else — another screenplay, something great — but it was never the same after that first one, too many rejections, and soon he had to find a job that paid the bills. An old college buddy helped him get an interview for a System Administrator position for "this certain website," and, before he knew what the site was about, he'd showed up for the interview and they'd liked him so much (and he'd really needed the money), he'd taken the job.

Things were never the same after that; he was working all the time; his marriage went cold. His Oxycontin addiction — which he'd nursed quietly and evenly since college — began to zag out of control; in the pornography industry he could get his pills cheaply and easily. And he drank, coming home from work in an angry haze only to nod off a couple of hours later on the couch with the TV left buzzing in the dark living room. And Jess drank with him, her way of coping with the growing distance between them. And they'd fight, screaming at each other over things neither of them could remember later. And, sometimes, Harlan would glance over during one of these fights and see Jake sitting up on the stairs watching them. Later, in the early morning haze, he'd remember Jake's face—dismayed eyes, tight-lipped mouth, dark bags no third grader should have to carry—and his heart would lurch painfully in his chest and he'd cry because he couldn't help himself, because he'd lost control of his life, because there were some things you could lose and never get back. Seeing his son like that, it was no wonder Jake had started the fire.

Harlan closed his laptop computer and sighed. He was having a hard time concentrating. It had only been eight months, although it felt much longer; he supposed he was still adjusting to life without opiates.

He told himself he wouldn't be feeling this way if Grace hadn't left him to go and find the makers of those strange videos; he hadn't heard from her in several days.

He stood, and walked out of the room and down the hallway. He looked out into the living room and his breath caught in his throat.

Oh, my God!

The two men were choking the woman, who began to writhe and struggle—one in his smiling drama mask, the other frowning—on the glowing television screen. Jake was a huddled lump sitting on the floor, his head craned backwards, transfixed before the scene.

Harlan lunged across the room and slammed the TV off, which blinked out with a flash and left the living room dark and silent except for his labored breathing.

"Jake! What do you think you're doing?"

His son looked up at him, his eyes large with wonder. "Wha...what was that?"

"Nothing. It's nothing. Just something horrible someone sent me. It's all fake — what those men were doing to that woman — you know that, don't you, Jake?"

"No. Not what the men were doing; that was just icky. What was going on behind them — "

"Just forget you ever saw it, okay? I know it's nasty, but it's all fake."

"But, Dad, what's going on *behind* the curtain is so much worse."

SIX

After her husband had sold his screenplay, and the royalty checks began to arrive in the mail, Harlan had begun to buy Jessica lots of things. That first Christmas, only eight months after the sale, she'd received an entire wardrobe of new clothes, a diamond bracelet, a brooch with an inset sapphire (because it looked good against her skin), several pairs of earrings, and various necklaces. She'd been flattered, and a little taken aback, not being the kind of girl who usually bothered with much jewelry. But at the time, Harlan hadn't cared which of the things she'd liked and which she didn't; he was just happy to make up for those first few years they'd been too poor to afford much more than two pairs of jeans each and a couple meager meals a day. (Together, the total sum of furniture they'd owned had been a bed frame and mattress, a couple of rickety end tables with chipped glass tops, a small dresser in pretty good shape they'd found by a cul-de-sac dumpster, and their aging Sony TV they kept propped on the dresser).

One of the things she got that Christmas, to go with all her new earrings and necklaces, was a small wire jewelry tree to hang them on. Harlan had helped their son pick it out and Jake had been thrilled to give it to her, practically jumping up and down as she opened it, his cheeks flushed a bright red against the huge grin he was unable to contain when she told him how much she liked the tree. It was an extravagant way to display her jewelry, with many different branches, each one with its own distinct curling offshoots, of various lengths and shapes, meeting into a single trunk that snaked down into a large and heavy base for support. In Jess's opinion, it was the nicest thing she received that Christmas and it remained standing (it was nearly impossible to knock over with a base so large and heavy) on the windowsill by the bed where she had put it the day her son had given it to her, draped with the colorful and shiny chains of things she rarely wore.

It was this jewelry tree she stared at now, its shadow casting an intricate pattern on the wall with the morning light, while she waited for Trevor, who slept silently next to her, to wake up. Trevor, who'd shown up on her doorstep that stormy evening a few days ago with a bouquet of flowers and a sly smile and greeted her like they'd only just seen each other the other day and never had that fight all those years ago...

*   *   *

"I'm sorry, Trevor, but I just don't feel the same things with you I feel with Harlan."

"What things?"

"You know, that warm fuzzy feeling: that connection."

Trevor is frowning. "I don't understand. I thought we were having fun."

"We were. We did. It's just," she struggles to find the right words, "it wasn't meant to be."

She shakes her head. "I have to go now. I'm sorry."

"No." He reaches out and takes hold of her arm. "You're mine, not his."

"I'm sorry, Trevor. Let me go."

"I don't think so."

"You're hurting me. I have to go."

"I don't think so."

She yanks her arm free.

"Don't you walk away from me, you bitch. Maybe it's time I laid down some ground rules."

And when she turns to leave, he grabs her again, his fingernails digging into the soft spots just below her shoulder joints. She cries out.

"You're mine. You'll always be mine. There's no getting out now."

With some effort, she turns to face him. She slaps him hard across the face. His grip loosens and she lunges across the room.

"You're a freak," she calls out to him as she leaves the room. "You're a…a pretentious zombie. Fuck off and leave me alone."

*   *   *

And that had been the end of it. She'd gone back to Harlan and hadn't seen Trevor until he'd shown up at her door unannounced. But that fight was years ago. She'd been angry; he'd been angry. She'd never meant to scream at him like that.

When Trevor, who was a very sound sleeper, finally stirred, she couldn't help herself—she'd been pondering Trevor's sudden appearance for days now and it was driving her crazy. She'd been dreaming about him. She'd been asking him questions in the hope he'd reveal something about the life he'd been leading, but his words had remained evasive and she was determined to get some answers out of him.

"Good morning," she said.

Trevor sat up in bed, looking out the window. He smiled. "Good morning."

"Uh, Trevor, honey? I know you just woke up, but I've been asking you about things and it's been driving me crazy." She wasn't making sense. She had to be direct. "What are you doing here?"

His smile never faltered. "I came to be with my girlfriend."

"Girlfriend? It's been years. How did you know where to find me?"

"Oh, I must have heard something somewhere."

"I'm not with Harlan anymore, did you know that? I signed the divorce papers a couple of weeks ago, but we've been separated for over a year. Aren't you curious about that? You never asked."

Trevor shrugged. "I must have heard about that somewhere as well. What would you say to some breakfast?"

She had to be firm. "Come on, Trevor. What have

you been doing all these years? You haven't told me a thing about your life. When I asked you earlier, all you said was you'd been traveling. Okay, where did you go? Who did you meet? What did you do?"

For a moment, his smile faltered the slightest bit. "I...I've been waiting. I've been waiting to come back to you."

Jess threw off the blankets and stood, exasperated. "You're impossible. How am I supposed to be with someone who won't share anything with me? And I don't mean those rambling stories of yours; I mean your actual experiences. If you've been somewhere, great. Tell me about it. I want to know." Tears sprung, stinging her eyes. "I don't want it to be like it was with Harlan. I want us to be able to communicate. I love you. Can't you see that? I want us to pick up where we left off. I...it's all happening so fast... but I do love you; I know I do, every time I look in your eyes. Please. Don't shut me out."

Trevor wore only the slightest of smiles now. "You love me? And you don't want to be with Harlan anymore?"

Jess choked back a sob. "No. I don't."

"You want to be with me?"

"Yes," she whispered. "Yes. I do."

Trevor's smile widened. "I love you too," he said.

Jess went to him and hugged him and he held her tight and they rocked together on the bed and then she looked deeply for a while into those dark eyes and she felt safe and calm and they made love and it was good.

*   *   *

"How are those pancakes coming?" Jess called from the dining room. She sat at the table sipping a screwdriver.

"Five minutes," Trevor called back from the kitchen.

From her spot at the head of the table she could see Trevor's taut butt flexing against the fabric of the shorts he wore. He was in very good shape for his age. Wherever he'd been, whatever he'd done, the world had been kind to him — not a wrinkle on him. He looked good.

It was strange really, when she thought about it; he looked just like the kid she'd dated in college — almost exactly like him. He even still had the same Members Only leather jacket he used to wear on their dates.

Jess took another sip of her screwdriver, then a gulp. Her drinking had slowed the past few days — she'd had other comforts and distractions — but just now she felt a little uneasy about things. She threw back the rest of her drink and set the glass down on the table. That strange feeling kept coming back.

Trevor still hadn't answered any of her questions.

SEVEN

On the car ride to school, in the backseat with Jesse — Jesse's mom driving, humming quietly to herself — they passed a little girl playing with something by the side of the street, poking the hairy lump with a blood-stained stick. It looked like she was giggling, but Jake was the only one who saw her. And then they'd passed by.

"What are you guys doing in school today?" Jesse's mom asked them.

"Nothing," Jesse answered.

"Oh, really? Nothing at all, huh?"

"We're talking about the Mayans and Aztecs today, Mrs. Oates," Jake said. "I think we're gonna get to make our own Mayan sacrificial temples out of sugar cubes."

"That sounds fun."

"Yeah."

Jesse's mom stopped the car by the curb in front of their school. "Okay, we're here. Have a good day at school, both of you."

"Bye, Mom."

"Bye, Mrs. Oates."

School was boring and uneventful.

*   *   *

"Hey, Jake. Can I see that game of yours again?"

"It's not done yet."

"That's okay. I just wanna see it."

They were walking home from school since Jesse's mom was stuck at work. They stopped and Jake dropped his backpack on the sidewalk, rummaging around inside it for his sketch pad. He pulled out the pad and flipped through a few random sketches — a dragon; an assortment of futuristic weapons and fire-arms; a depiction of "The battle of the stick-figures," complete with explosions and flying heads — stopped on the page he'd been working on in school today, and handed the pad over to Jesse.

Jesse looked over the map-sketch Jake had made: a winding cave, the entrance a giant yawning skull. "Man, I wish I could draw like you can. What's this?"

"That's the pit you fall down at the beginning of the game into the darkness at the bottom. Then you have to find your way out."

"But how is it gonna work?"

"This is just the sketch. I'm gonna make a game board and you'll roll dice and collect equipment and stuff. It'll be fun; you'll see."

"What're those guys?" Jesse pointed to a pair of

dancing figures near the top of the page, one grinning fiercely, the other frowning sternly.

"Oh, those are the Fuggle Brothers. You don't want to run into them. They do the bidding of the Man Behind the Curtain."

"Who's the Man Behind the Curtain?"

"He hides in the dark and if he catches you he kills you and you have to start the game over."

Jesse frowned. "What does he look like?"

"He can look like whoever he wants to look like. He's, like, a magician, or something, behind his curtain of shadow."

"So how do you beat him?"

"You can't."

"That's stupid. There has to be some way to kill the bad guy. How do you win the game?"

"The first person to escape the cave wins."

Jesse looked more closely at the Fuggle Brothers. "Huh. Okay."

Jake took his drawing pad back from Jesse.

A shadow fell over them.

"You boys weren't thinking of trampling through my yard, were you?"

They looked up and Old Man Greene was standing on the edge of his yard, holding his broom like he might try and sweep them off the sidewalk.

"No, Mr. Greene."

"Uh-huh." Old Man Greene didn't look convinced. "You better get along now, alright."

Jake and Jesse continued their walk, taking the long way around the corner, around Old Man Greene's precious lawn.

They passed by Mrs. Marlow's yard and all those

weird gnomes that seemed to follow you with their eyes as you passed.

"Hey, do you think I could come over tonight and play video games or something?" Jake asked his friend.

"Not tonight. My grandparents are coming over for dinner and my mom says I have to take a bath and wear my stupid church clothes and look 'presentable'." Jesse sighed. "I'll try and be on Call of Duty later, though, if you want to try and catch me online."

"Okay."

They walked in silence for a couple of minutes. Jake kicked absently at a pine cone.

"Why do you want to come over tonight anyway?" Jesse asked. "Tonight's a school night."

"I know, it's just my mom's dating this new guy and I think they're going out and I'll be stuck with Johnny the Babysitter."

Jesse looked at Jake incredulously. "Your mom's dating already? Didn't your parents just get divorced?"

Jake shrugged. "Yeah, but I guess she knew him from college or something."

Jesse shook his head. "Whatever."

"I don't like him very much. He smells funny."

"I wouldn't like some freak dating my mom either."

Jake kicked another pine cone, sending it skidding into the street.

*   *   *

"Really? Did you hear Cheryl was flirting with Kevin Oberman at Carl's party last weekend? Oh, yeah? Fucking crazy, right?"

Jake dropped into the couch and flicked through the channels on the TV. He wished his mom didn't still feel it was necessary for him to have a babysitter—he was old enough to take care of himself—especially one like Johnny. If only Johnny would get off the phone and shut the hell up.

Johnny laughed, louder than was necessary. "I know. Kevin Oberman is such a douche, but so is the whole fucking track team. All those guys are total D-bags. You know they're just going to get their asses handed to them again this year." A pause. "Oh, hell yeah. Those are some nice legs. Uh-huh. Let me put it this way: I wouldn't mind bending Cheryl over the hood of my car, if you know what I mean. She'd love it, too. You know she would; screaming like there was no tomorrow."

More laughter. Jake tried to block out Johnny's annoying voice and focus on something else. There was an anti-meth commercial on the TV: a man wandering through the desert, his face decaying in time-lapse, skin turning yellow and blotchy, teeth browning, gray gums pulling away to a leering husk of a face; eyes vacant and glazed.

Jake looked away, dropping the remote on the couch next to him.

Johnny, immediately, snatched up the remote and began flipping the channels without any consideration for what Jake was watching. "What channel is it? Really? I didn't know you liked that kind of shit?"

The TV blinked a few times, and then stopped on

a scene of a woman running through a park at night, panting and moaning in apparent terror.

"Eh, they're pretty nice. Not bad, I guess."

The woman was running, her bosom heaving in the half-torn T-shirt that clung to her, skin-tight.

"Yeah-yeah, I know. I agree. Nice rack. I've seen better."

Jake watched the woman on the screen; he didn't think he'd ever understand what the big deal was. It was just a woman running through a park. So what?

Then there were growls and a small group of zombies staggered from beneath the shadows of the trees. The woman turned, looked at the decaying faces behind her, and screamed, renewing her vigorous run.

Jake shook his head. What was this crap?

The next shot was a close-up of the woman's face.

Jake's heart began to pound; his breath caught in his throat.

It was his mom. It couldn't be his mom. No way. But it was. And she was trapped, backed into a dark corner. The dead people closing in, closer and closer.

Jake slammed his hands over his eyes; he didn't want to see this.

He peeked through his fingers.

The zombies swarmed over the woman (his mom!), clawing and groaning; a spurt of blood; wet sucking sounds.

Jake ran from the room, up the stairs, down the hall, slamming his bedroom door. He sank to the floor, panting, his breath hitching in his throat. He heard Johnny stomping up the stairs and down the hall.

"Hey, kid, you okay in there?"

"Fine," he called through the door. "I'm just…I'm fine, okay?"

"Yeah. Alright."

Johnny, still on the phone, his footsteps receding: "This kid's a fucking nutcase, I tell you. He just ran out of the room. Scared over that zombie movie, I guess. Uh-huh. Uh…he's in grade school. I don't know. Twelve, or something…"

Jake waited to catch his breath. It was just a movie; he had no reason to be afraid. He'd seen worse, much worse.

After a minute or two, he felt a little calmer. He knew the woman he'd seen on the TV wasn't really his mom, but, he had to admit to himself, he'd lost it there for a second—he'd been so sure it was her.

Jake shivered. He hoped his mom wasn't in some kind of trouble.

EIGHT

He'd received a third video, coming home from work last night; it'd been sitting there on his doorstep waiting for him, same as the other ones. Getting this video at the door, sitting down to watch it, was not like putting on one of his horror movies—that morbid, unreal feeling that came over him when he watched the creepy, the disturbing, and the grotesque; as long as he always knew in the back of his mind the difference between reality and fiction—had been more like sitting down to a funeral, his blood pounding in his temples, his hands shaky and clammy with perspiration. He'd flicked the DVD player closed, sat down, and hit play on the remote.

Static. Then that room again, with the stone table and the red curtain.

He watched and waited for a woman and the two masked men to appear, for the torturing to begin.

Two minutes passed. Three. Nothing changed in the room. Then, more static.

He watched the video again, remembering what Jake had said about something being behind the curtain. He looked closely, tried to see, but there was nothing; maybe there was some movement in the curtain, but the video quality was too poor to be certain. He watched it two more times, just to be sure, and found nothing.

Still, it made him uneasy. Where were these things coming from? Why didn't the people sending them want him to know who they were? And days had gone by without a word from Grace. Had he gotten the wrong impression about their relationship? Had her saying she was going in search of the filmmakers somehow been her way of telling him she didn't want to see him anymore? He didn't think so. Why hadn't she called?

Harlan shut the door on his shelf of movies. He'd been considering what movie to watch, scanning his collection, but he realized now he didn't feel like watching anything he had. Instead, maybe he'd have another drink; tonight he felt like getting completely shit-faced. And fuck getting any work done. Tonight, he wanted to wash away that uneasy feeling inside him, that feeling that he was losing control of his life again, that feeling that he wasn't entirely himself anymore. Tonight, he'd get wasted, and tomorrow, he'd be too hung-over to care how lonely and scared he was beginning to feel.

A bottle of bourbon was in the kitchen, as was his old fashioned glass. He poured generously: three fingers, for starters. Gulped it down. Then three fingers more. And the haze began to close over him.

* * *

Harlan woke slowly; face down on a couch pillow, an uncomfortable crease pushing painfully across his cheek. His head was a hot fever of dull pain. His mind swirled with images of his son, and his ex-wife, and a small silver lighter, and the old house, and Jake's school, and Grace; dreams—sloshing incoherently back and forth within the confines of his skull, back and forth and around like a relentless tide.

He couldn't remember a thing from the last ten hours of his life—not that there was likely anything worth remembering.

"Fuck," Harlan mumbled, peeling his cheek from the pillow and raising himself. "Oh, fuck," he pushed the palms of his hands into his hot and throbbing forehead.

He held himself gingerly on the couch and slowly turned his head to look around the living room.

The first thing he noticed: his entertainment center, which he was usually very careful to keep organized and clean, gaped open, its doors flung ruthlessly to either side, one hanging limply from a single hinge, the other torn free completely. His movies spilled from their shelves, thrown about, no doubt, in the haphazard randomness of a drunken fugue. The bottle of bourbon, which had begun the night sealed and filled with its amber liquid at the liquor store, now lay tumbled sideways on the carpeted floor at the middle of a dark stain, empty of all but the final dregs of faded backwash. And his coffee table was strewn with various kitchen utensils, mostly knives, and—he groaned inside to see this—it looked as if he'd carved a little message to himself in the wooden surface; it read: "Harlan was here," and his name was underlined with progressively more jagged and violent scratches. And...

Harlan froze, his heart like a rock in his chest. There was a blank DVD case sitting atop the torn remains of its plain brown paper wrapping. His television was on, broadcasting static into the morning-lit room.

Another video. And he'd watched it, apparently. He tried to think, to remember how the video had come to him and what it had shown him, but his mind was useless oatmeal-batter expanding in his head. His body shook. What had happened last night? What had he been doing?

He didn't have a choice really: he had to watch the video. Maybe it would all come flooding back to him, his memory, like it did for people in the movies. The remote lay amongst the knives on his coffee table; he grabbed it with a trembling hand. He hit the play button.

The screen flickered; the image came into focus. The room presented itself as it always did—the shimmering red curtain, the tiled floor, the stone table, which was an altar he now realized—and a woman walked confidently into the scene, her hair a tousle of blonde curls falling on her shoulders. The woman was completely naked, older than the last couple of girls, and she was smiling, a sardonic smirk. She took a seat on the altar and waited.

A moment passed; the woman leaned forward and looked into the camera, and even before she winked, Harlan knew who she was. His stomach sank; he felt sick. Grace had done more than just find the filmmakers; she'd taken a starring role in one of their films.

Harlan watched; his mouth dry and bitter like chalk powder.

The two men came into the scene, grinning and frowning respectively. They tied Grace to the altar. The grinning man produced a whip. Grace screamed, a flaming red welt-line appearing across her mid-riff. Grace writhed. The grinning man whipped her again. The frowning man slid his belt from his waist and joined his companion, the thick leather like the dull thwack of an open-palmed slap.

Harlan cringed from his place on the couch.

After a while, the men stopped, dropping their whipping implements. The frowning man pulled Grace roughly into place so that her legs dropped over the side of the table, her pale ass-cheeks spread for the camera. The men took turns fucking her. Grace moaned, whether in pleasure or pain, it was difficult to tell; Harlan couldn't see her face.

After both men had finished, leaving their seed dripping down Grace's leg, they pulled her to a sitting position, facing the camera. The grinning man stood on one side; the frowning man stood on the other. Grace lifted her free hand — shaking notice-ably — to the camera, as if to assure Harlan she was okay. She looked worn and old.

Then, the frowning man took up his belt again, made a noose, and put it over Grace's neck. She tried to smile; a dark bruise wrapped one of her eyes. The man pulled the noose tight. Grace sputtered; she struggled halfheartedly, because that was what she was supposed to do. Then she stopped for a moment. Her eyes turned to the frowning man. She renewed her struggles, more forcefully this time, more realistically, panicked. She brought her free hand up and tried to pull the belt away from her neck. The grinning man stepped in to help restrain her. Grace's hand beat at the frowning man's face. Her legs kicked wildly, then began to slump.

Harlan couldn't pull his eyes away; he was in shock. Grace's struggles looked real. In unison, their heads turned, slowly, facing the camera, looking out at him — the grinning man and the frowning man — Grace lying motionless on the stone altar between them.

Blank screen. Static.

*   *   *

Later, Harlan was sick. He spent the morning heaving and vomiting. The afternoon was spent with another bottle. He didn't know what else to do.

NINE

Jessica tossed her car keys on the kitchen counter and lowered her grocery bag to the granite surface. Trevor was in the other room watching TV. She upended the bag, using her free hand to keep her purchases from rolling off the counter: a dozen tiny plastic bottles drumming on the polished rock.

She peeked in on Trevor. He was sitting upright in the middle of the couch, staring at the TV.

"What are you watching," she asked him.

"Nothing," he answered.

She left him to zone out. He'd been distant. They didn't talk much. Their relationship seemed to be crumbling before it had even begun.

She picked one of the bottles from the counter; she liked the feel of the cool, sweating plastic. She flicked the little red cap off between her thumb and index finger and the vodka was a freezing burn running down her throat, settling in her chest and expanding. She sighed and tossed the empty in the trash. She'd been drinking pretty heavily the past couple of days, but Trevor didn't seem to notice or care.

She downed another bottle, then slid a couple more, one into each side of the front pocket of her drooping sweatshirt, and went to join Trevor on the couch. Jake was in school; she was living on her settlement from the divorce; what was Trevor doing? He didn't work; that was obvious. He didn't do anything. He slept twelve hours a night. He made meals. He talked, but haltingly, and only about college and the things they'd done together years ago. *Remember the time I brought you a bouquet of flowers, on our sixteenth date I believe, and when you went to smell them a grasshopper jumped out and nearly scared you half to death?* Random anecdotes. *Remember when you decided to teach me how to kiss because you said I used too much tongue and then, after that, I didn't use enough tongue?* And he never laughed. *Remember when you slipped on something greasy in the Student Union Building on our fifth date and we were holding hands and you pulled me down so we both ended up on the floor?* At first she'd laughed and enjoyed doing most of the talking, but now, she was beginning to find Trevor's behavior odd. The Trevor she knew had been smooth and charming. This Trevor still had the looks of her old boyfriend from college, but something had changed; he didn't seem the same.

She took a seat on the couch; she could feel the alcohol warming her blood. "What should we do tonight? You want to go out?"

His eyes never left the glowing television screen.

"If you'd like."

"I don't mind you living here," she said, sighing. "But, don't you need to go and get a job or something?"

"I'd rather not."

She had to try again. "Trevor, honey," she began, "what did you say you were doing before this?"

His eyes remained frozen to television set. "I already told you. I was traveling."

She had to press him; she had to try. "But what about work? What were you doing to make money?"

"I wasn't working. I didn't worry about money."

She gripped one of the bottles in her pocket. "I know you weren't rich. Wasn't your dad a welder or something? Where did you get the money to travel for all those years?"

There was little inflection in Trevor's voice. "Years? I guess it was—"

"Hey, come on," Jess could feel herself getting frustrated with Trevor's apathetic and evasive attitude, "why don't you turn the damn TV off and talk to me?"

Trevor didn't move.

Jess took the bottle from her pocket, discarded the cap, and emptied it down her throat. She swallowed, gasped lightly, and snatched the TV remote from its spot on the couch between her and Trevor. She switched the TV off and, the anger suddenly boiling up within her, threw the remote across the room; it thudded against the wall and its cover and batteries spewed out across the floor like the guts from a small rodent.

"Fuck you, Trevor," she screamed. "Why won't

you talk to me? What the fuck is wrong with you?"

The tiny empty bottle tumbled to the floor.

Trevor didn't move, didn't stir. Instead, he sat staring at the misty black TV screen. "What do you mean?"

Jess stood. She stepped in front of Trevor so that she was in between him and the television set. "Trevor. Hey. Look at me." Trevor's eyes flickered and then met hers. "There you are. What's going on? Where have you been?"

"Traveling." His eyes were black pits. "Can't you see that? Now leave me alone. We can go to dinner later."

Jess took a step back. She felt flushing heat burning her cheeks. She tore the other bottle from her sweatshirt and swallowed it down. The heat churned her confidence and her anger.

Fuck this, she thought.

She slapped him hard across the cheek. She didn't know she was going to do it until after, her palm stinging, her nerves bristling with the feel of his beard stubble.

Trevor's head swiveled to meet her astonished gaze. His facial expression remained a glazed blank; his eyes spilled inky blackness.

She couldn't pull her eyes away from his. "Remember that time in college on our twenty-sixth date when you slapped me and called me a...what was it? I don't remember now. What was it you called me?" His eyes. What was wrong with his eyes? Something stirred: dropped cream in a cup of coffee. For the first time since he'd materialized on her doorstep, she saw a level of intelligence in him she hadn't seen before.

And she saw rage.

Jess took another step back. "Trevor…what…"

"No," he growled. "You're mine, not his."

"What are you talking about? Trevor, you're scaring me."

His hand shot forward, gripping her bicep painfully, drawing her into his reeking breath. "I don't think so."

She tried to keep her breathing level. "You're hurting me, Trevor," she said. "Let me go."

"I don't think so."

She yanked her arm away and began to back off. He stood; his mouth twitched; grinned.

"Don't walk away from me, you bitch," he said. "Maybe it's time I laid down some ground rules."

She turned to flee. He reached for her: she could feel his fingernails digging at the soft flesh just below her shoulder blade, twitching at her skin to sink deep and pull her back to him like a stuck trout.

"You're mine. You'll always be mine. There's no getting out now."

Jess lunged free, groping past the couch towards the stairs, Trevor behind her, his breath rasping like a lecherous animal. Then she was tripping on the stairs, climbing up hand over hand, each stair like a rung on a ladder. He was slavering behind her, blathering after her in that voice that was deeper and louder than Trevor's—she could feel him close, swiping at the empty air just behind the back of her head.

At the top of the stairs she risked a glance over her shoulder. Trevor was at the bottom looking up at her. His face contorted with expression. His eyes flared. He was shaking his head back and forth—

slowly — back and forth.

"Stay away from me, Trevor. I don't know what's wrong with you. Just…stay away."

Trevor's mouth jerked into a jack-o-lantern of teeth and there was not a doubt in Jess's mind he intended murder. "You're mine. You'll always be mine. There's no getting out now. If I can't have you…" He shrugged.

Jess turned, and fled down the hallway. She tripped, sprawled, gained her feet. Trevor's presence was like a muggy stirring of air pushing behind her. She grasped the doorknob and pushed through, tumbling into Jake's room — because it was at the end of the hallway — kicked the door closed, and thrust herself up against it, twisting the lock.

Her own breathing was a raspy panic. She expected Trevor to try the knob, to push and jiggle the door. Nothing. She couldn't hear him. It was silence except for her shuddering breath.

After a moment, she couldn't tell how long: a light knocking, a tapping knuckle on the other side of the door.

"That's okay," the strange voice said. "I'll wait."

Jess slumped on the floor against the door. She was trapped. She closed her eyes, forcing her breathing to slow; she could see dots exploding and wriggling behind her eyelids. She was scared and confused. Her brain bobbed in her swelling vodka intoxication. She needed a moment.

"When does Jake get home?"

Her eyes shot open.

"Where's my son?" the voice breathed.

TEN

Come with me, Jake. Come and see.

On his walk back from school, Jake took his time. Jesse had soccer practice on Wednesdays and so he was by himself. He was curious about something he'd seen on the car ride to school that morning. In the back seat he'd been peering out—watching the neighborhood scroll by, like he always did when Jesse's mom gave him a ride to school—when they'd passed by Mrs. Marlow's yard and he thought he saw one of her garden gnomes wink at him. He'd whipped his head around and looked hard out the window, but the gnome's face and eyes, of course, had only been painted and immovable plastic. Then his eyes had been caught by another pair of gnomes, just as the car—and his view of the yard—was passing around the next curve: these two arranged in an inappropriate position, one bent before the other, both smiling wickedly. He wanted to see if these gnomes were still arranged this way, or if Mrs. Marlow had noticed the joke some kids from his school had probably played on her garden setup.

Come and see, Jake. Come and see.

That voice—those whispered words, the cadence of each syllable, each word crisp and meaningful—was so real to him, even through the fading haze of his dream from the night before. He felt the authority of that voice, understood its urgency, even if he didn't understand its purpose. But it was only a dream, and he understood the childishness of dreams, that they were only as real as the images on the TV, reflections of the truth maybe, but unimportant in the real world. He was old enough to be able to tell the difference between what was real and what wasn't.

And so, he walked slowly, looking about at his surroundings as he went, mindful of what he saw, of the richness of color and detail. The afternoon was warm and pleasant. The sky above was a drifting cathedral of gradating blue, cloudless and vast. Beneath him, the sidewalk was a gray and even path. A large tree shaded him as he passed, its trunk the size of a small Elvin house, bark like skin that had been ripped and flayed and dried to jerky, roots crawling from the ground, the branches and leaves above a looming canopy of darkened green. Cars passed; their whooshing passage and speed unimportant on an afternoon like this. He passed the spot where he thought he'd seen a little girl poking a dead animal with a stick a few days ago, but there was no sign of the furry carcass and he had no way to be sure. A little ways ahead lay a small pile of discarded boards he made a mental note to come back later and collect for use on his tree house. He walked the long way around Old Man Greene's lawn and marveled at its deep green hue. He was saddened to see a single spot of churned earth, like a gopher's mound but larger, in the middle of all that perfect grass. He knew Old Man Greene put a lot of work into his lawn and he knew how angry Greene would be when he saw the dug-up spot. It had probably been kids from his school, like Brad Falchuck or that fatass Tim Curry, who'd ruined Old Man Greene's lawn; there were always kids like that who found wrecking and destroying the things other people cared about the funniest thing in the world.

When he reached Mrs. Marlow's yard, he was not disappointed. There seemed to be more gnomes than before; it looked as if Mrs. Marlow had found a few more of the plastic staring figures to add to her collection. They peered from behind bushes and took crouching positions amongst the tulips and daffodils; along the line of irises, and frolicked in the roses. And on the side of the yard, behind a half-barrel potter of bobbing lilies, the two gnomes continued their salacious act. Frozen in positions of action, both gnomes wore duplicate expressions of glazed happiness, with, Jake could see as he stared, perhaps a touch of mischievousness.

Jake continued on his way with a smile on his face. There were a lot of things in this world he didn't understand, but it was funny to see the gnomes like that. He thought his dad would have found it funny too.

He dug his key out of his pocket more out of habit than necessity, as he walked up through the front yard of his house; his mom was always home now since she'd separated from his dad and quit her job at the salon; the front door would be unlocked.

He reached forward and the door swung open before he could touch it. His mom's boyfriend was standing in the entryway grinning at him. "Hello, son," the man said to him, "we have things to discuss."

Jake stepped into the house. "Uh, hi."

Trevor stepped aside. "Come in, Jake." Then, almost gleefully, "Please, do come in."

Jake shook his head. It felt, suddenly, as if he'd just stepped into a patch of fog and his senses were reeling, needing a moment to catch his bearings and reorient himself to his surroundings. He faded out for a moment, and then came back.

"Please, take a seat at the table. Would you like something to drink? Coke? A juice perhaps?"

"No," Jake said. "No, thanks." He let his backpack drop to the floor and sat in one of the chairs at the dining room table.

His mom's boyfriend, Trevor, slid into the chair across from his. He continued to smile. Jake's gaze wandered uncomfortably over the man's shoulders, looking at the stairway behind him, at the array of family photographs on the walls, at the hutch and his mom's doll collection peering through its glass panels like doomed prisoners.

"Jake," Trevor said to him. "I have some important things to tell you and they're not going to be easy to hear."

Jake met Trevor's dark, steady gaze, then dropped

it to his hands picking numbly at a hangnail on the table.

"Still," the man said, "I think you're the right age to hear it." He leaned close across the table. "You're not like the other little boys."

Jake kept his eyes on his fidgeting hands.

"You're different, Jake. Special. You can do things others can't. You know this to be true; you can feel it inside your heart."

Jake shook his head.

"Yes," the man said. "You can. I can teach you things; show you things. That's why I'm here."

"Where's my mom?"

"She's upstairs. Don't worry about her now. She's fine."

Jake looked up. For the first time, he took in this man's appearance: a young man still, he couldn't tell how old, but younger than his mom, with slightly wild auburn hair, large, even eyes, tanned skin with a rugged spray of gunslinger-like beard stubble, and full lips, peeled back to show off a full array of large, perfect teeth.

And he had to catch his breath because his mom was standing half-way down the stairs with her finger to her lips, signaling him to be quiet.

"Jake. Look at me."

He returned his eyes to Trevor's, afraid he'd given away his mom's position, but Trevor didn't seem to have noticed.

"I want to show you something. Will you let me show you something?"

Jake's mom was at the bottom of the stairs. She held a large and awkward object in one hand, with protruding limbs that cast an ugly shadow on the wall behind her from the fading light of the day.

Trevor stood, holding his hand out. "Come with me, Jake. Come and see."

Jake held his breath. He felt frozen in place, body and mind, unsure what to think; numbed. Before him on the table, his hands grappled with each other painfully.

"Haven't you always wondered, Jake? Haven't you always imagined?"

His mom lifted the tangled-looking thing above her head.

"There are such wonders beneath the surface of things. I can show you worlds, Jake. Worlds! Come with me!"

The sound, as the tangled and heavy thing came down on the back of Trevor's head, was sickeningly loud, the unreal crack of breaking balls in the pool games Jake's dad used to watch on television on lazy Sunday afternoons, only wet. Trevor's eyes glazed to black and his body crumpled, as if his muscles had turned gelatinous and his mass had no other choice than to submit to gravity and thud to the floor.

Jake remained frozen as he watched the dark stain bloom in the rug around Trevor's head. The tangled thing—the jewelry tree Jake had given to his mom for Christmas a couple of years ago—sat upright on the floor nearby; its outreaching branches seemed to vibrate with violent energy.

His mom stood with her trembling hands held out before her. "Jake? Honey? Are you okay?"

Jake remained sitting at the table, his mind mired in foggy surreality. He didn't know what to think.

"Yeah, Mom." He felt shocked and sticky. "I think so."

His mom came to him and he stood and let her hug him tight and she kissed him on the top of his head over and over and she kept saying everything was going to be alright and not to worry and everything was going to be alright.

"You bitch," that voice said behind them.

His mom shrieked.

They turned and Trevor was sitting up, his head slightly misshapen on one side. He stood on unsure legs, his eyes running with milky swirls against the black, coming into focus.

*　　*　　*

Jessica pushed herself between her son and Trevor.

Trevor brought his hands up to strangle her and lurched forward.

Jess snatched the jewelry tree from the floor and brought it across her body in a wide sweep, gashing jagged lines of flesh from Trevor's contempt-filled face, but Trevor was unmoved by the wounds, his hands finding her neck, tightening suddenly and forcefully before she had a chance to snatch her next breath. Dark spots twirled at the edges of her vision and she could hear her son wailing helplessly.

Trevor's face leered close to hers, a flap of cheek hanging open to a line of bleached molars, his eyes brimming with dark violence, with finality.

She lifted the jewelry tree; it was heavy, too heavy. She brought it up. She could feel her strength leaving her, flowing out of her body and into the ether. The jewelry tree came down, she had little strength left to put behind it, but it came down nonetheless, jagged branches spearing into Trevor's upturned face.

*   *   *

Jake was scarcely aware of the sound leaking out of him — his panicked wail; watching his mom lift the jewelry tree and bring it down, a protruding branch piercing one of Trevor's eyes and digging deep into the softness there. He watched his mom fall free, dropping to her knees, and Trevor fall onto his back in a pool of his own blood.

His mom grunted and gasped, lifting the wiry tree. She brought it down. Lifted. Brought it down. Again and again, until Jake ran to her and screamed at her to stop.

The jewelry tree was a wriggling tangle of wires hung with gore, toppled on its side. Trevor's face was a cavernous stain, a single fracture of bone protruding glaringly from the mess.

Jake and his mom slumped helplessly on the floor nearby in each other's arms, spattered with and a part of the mess. They held each other tight and cried, and Jake let the fog close over his mind for a time as he forgot about things.

When he opened his eyes next he was alone on the floor and he could hear his mom on the phone in the kitchen.

Come, Jake, the voice wafted through his mind. *Come and see.*

PART TWO: DREAMS

ELEVEN

Jake had always been small for his age, but three years ago, when he'd been in first grade, he'd been the smallest kid in his class. His walks to and from school back then had been faster, with more exuberance; he'd enjoyed skipping along, brandishing sticks he'd pick from the ground like swords, swiping the heads from the milkweeds as he passed.

It had been on one of these walks that he'd, by chance, kicked something shiny and plastic in his eager shuffle to get home to his afternoon cartoons. The bright orange thing skipped once against the sidewalk and flew into a cluster of bushy weeds by the side of the street. Curious, he'd taken his knees and fetched the object from the tangles. It was orange and oval with a steel striker on one end: a cigarette lighter. And, after a few failed attempts to run his thumb over the wheel without success — his hands being too small for the task—he managed to produce a flame by holding the lighter in one hand and rolling the striker across the palm of the other. The flame was tiny and insignificant in the brightness of the afternoon sun, almost invisible. He dropped the lighter into his pocket and immediately forgot about it, skipping all the rest of the way home.

That night, discarding his jeans to the floor of his bedroom as he prepared for bed, the bright orange lighter had slipped from his pants pocket and his mom would have seen it if he hadn't quickly kicked it aside with one sock-covered foot. The lighter spun into the cavernous region under his bed and his mom tucked him in and he'd fallen into sleep with excitement over the fact that he'd found something his best friend Jesse would find fascinating.

The next day, in the corner of the playground at recess where the teachers couldn't see what they were doing, he'd brought the lighter out for Jesse to see.

"That's cool. Does it work?" Jesse asked him.

"Yeah, it does. You want to meet after school and we can go burn some things?"

"Okay. Where?"

"I'll meet you in Sherwood Forest."

*   *   *

Behind the school, past the playground, where the drainage creek separated the suburban middle-class homes from the apartment complexes, there was a patch of forested area known as Sherwood Forest. It wasn't a very large patch of ground—one could walk from one side to the other in just a few minutes—but the denseness of the cottonwood trees and oak bushes gave it a wilderness quality that was, to a child of six years, a joy to find so close to home and in the middle of the city.

Jake spent many hours in Sherwood Forest, playing games with Jesse, building forts, and wandering about by himself.

*   *   *

That afternoon, Jake met Jesse amongst the trees, and they collected scraps of newspaper, fast food wrappers and twigs, and burned all these things. They watched the flames with a fascination as old as humanity itself, entranced by the ephemeral flickering dance of the flame. They paraded about their makeshift stone circle hearth, whooping and pounding the earth with their feet. When they looked up at the sky and realized the sky was dimming and it was getting late, they stamped out their tiny fire, hurriedly kicked sand over the charred remains, flung their backpacks over their shoulders, and headed for home.

After that, on his daily walks, Jake began to notice other discarded lighters and packets of matches, where he'd never noticed them before. He found a blue lighter and a black one, but had to throw the black one away because the striker wheel was missing. He found a packet of matches with the squiggly words "Lou's Emporium" etched in green across a manila background with three matches still left inside. He found another lighter with a woman's face on it, her finger pushed up against her pursed lips as if telling him to be quiet, not to tell anyone, that this was their little secret. Another pack of matches he found — almost full, with only a couple of matches torn out — advertising a place called the "Nevermore Ranch." He found several other lighters of various colors and styles. He began a collection, stashing his findings in the small hollow of an old tree stump in Sherwood Forest.

Then, one day when he was bored and alone, Jake wandered down to Sherwood Forest on a Saturday. After spending the better part of the morning hauling old wooden planks and boards that had washed up along the creek into the forest for tree house building supplies, he was tired and sweaty and it was approaching lunch time; he was hungry. But before heading home, he threaded his way through the reedy undergrowth — using a stick to keep the branches back, that, if you were not careful, would whip you in the face as you passed — to a small alcove of dense foliage where the dead stump of an ancient tree, hollowed out by rot and a host of small animals over the years, now housed his collection of lighters and matches. He was scared to light the matches; he was too afraid of burning himself to be able to hold his fingers close enough to the match head to strike it effectively. He'd ruined many of the flimsy matches trying, rending them to scraps as he attempted to scrape the cardboard over the dark striker strip. He was, however, able to use a couple of the lighters to produce a flame he could put to the scraps of trash he'd been collecting, and, sometimes, he'd catch himself staring at the little nub of flame at the end of the lighter until the metal burned his fingers and he dropped the lighter into the underbrush with a yelp. Other times, without Jesse to warn him against it, he'd light a small pile of papers and dried pine needles and watch the flames expand and cavort. He found the flame intensely fascinating, in a way he couldn't describe; he could feel his face going slack, sweat beading his forehead and upper lip, the flare of excitement running up his throat, warming his chest. He lost himself in its efforts, his thoughts pushed from his mind, his brain like a raw and over-charged jelly. He'd stare, until the flames grew and crept from their spot of containment, and he had to shake himself from his trance, and stomp out the flames.

Until that one day, when Jesse had been otherwise occupied and he'd discovered a method for striking the soft matches between the striker strip and the bent-over cover of the matchbook, lighting the entire book, each match head hissing to life for a moment like striking snakes; then he'd dropped the inflamed matchbook into the grass by the tree stump, and his stash, and sat to watch the flames expand in the underbrush.

For a moment, he forgot whom and where he was.

The next moment, he's blinking in disbelief at the fire, at the wall of curling orange snakes hissing and crackling and gnawing at the reedy bushes right in front of him. How could the flames grow so fast? What could he do? He'd lost control, he realized; it seeped into his awareness. The skin on his face and hands felt sore and sun-burnt.

He ran. He had to get help. He ran to the only place he knew. He ran all the way home as fast as he could, bursting through the door screaming: "Mom!"

Screaming: "Dad!"

His dad was on the couch watching TV. He said, "What's up, Jake? What's wrong?"

In his head, he could see Sherwood Forest in flames, the fire dancing through the dried winter grass up to the soccer field, eager for a taste of his school. And, even though he wouldn't mind missing school, the thought of his actions being responsible for burning it down terrified him.

"I..." he stuttered to his dad. He could feel tears stinging his eyes. "Dad, I did something bad..."

His Dad stood and came over to him, clearly concerned. "What did you do?"

Through the tears he managed to get his message across. "Fire...Sherwood Forest..."

In the backseat of the car—his dad driving, his mom in the passenger's seat—he can't keep back his tears as they speed down the street. His dad is yelling into his cell phone at the fire department. His mom is freaking out, talking a mile a minute about responsibilities, and being careful, and playing by himself, and how they were so busy telling him to watch out for sex predators they forgot to mention he shouldn't "burn the fucking neighborhood down." He's never heard his mom—his dad a few times, but not his mom—use that word before, but he hears it now: "*Fucking.*"

The fire department was right down the block from the school so that by the time they got to the scene the flashing red trucks had pulled up to the school and the firemen had already strung a couple of hoses across the playground and were spraying Sherwood Forest in prismatic mist.

Jake was not allowed out of the backseat so what he heard through the cracked car window was his father grumble, "I don't see a fire," and his mom, "They must have caught it in time."

Later, his dad told him he could have "burned the whole goddamn neighborhood to the ground," and he was grounded for two weeks.

A few weeks later, he ventured back to Sherwood Forest, and when he did, he was surprised to discover only a small burned out spot where the old log used to be.

Eventually, his parents forgave him, figuring he'd learned his lesson and would never do something like that again—and he didn't plan on playing with fire anymore. But something changed. He had nightmares: the world burned, and he didn't want to see that there was more to all this than simple coincidence, that when he caught sight of a flickering flame his eyes were pulled towards it, that there was more to see, and unknown forces to show him what was beneath the surface of things, and he just didn't want to see any of it.

TWELVE

The phone call woke him up. He'd been sleeping on the couch and he realized he still hadn't cleaned his apartment; what time was it? He struggled to sit up and the world was driven by a drunken sea captain, swaying and falling. He clutched his forehead: feverish and sticky. He gripped the arm of the couch and stands. His cell phone was sitting on the coffee table amongst numerous beer and liquor bottles, but the entire table seemed to buckle outwards and away. He fell to his knees before it, the bottles chiming, and his cell phone was cold and hard in his sweating palm.

He flipped his phone open. "Hello?" his voice husked from a great distance.

"Harlan? Is that you? You sound strange."

He tried to clear his throat. "Jess?"

"Would you come over? Please? Jake and I need your help. Okay? Please?"

"Now?"

"Right now."

His head throbbed. "Sure."

"And, Harlan?"

"What?"

"Please don't call the cops."

"Why would I…" but the phone goes dead.

He shoved his phone in his pocket. Why the fuck would *he* call the cops? *Those fucks were worthless anyway*, he thought. When he'd tried to call them about what happened to Grace all they could tell him was some bullshit about a seventy-two hour waiting period on missing persons. When had he made that call? How long had it been?

Harlan ripped his phone back out of his pocket and stared at the date. Shit. He was losing it. He needed to cut back on his drinking; he was having some serious blackout issues. He'd never taken anything so hard—not his divorce, not his mother's death, nothing—but watching Grace choked to death, over and over again, was something else. He could see the images even now—her eyes turning upwards at the smiling man to see if her performance had been satisfactory, her panicked struggles as she realized what was really happening, her terror-frozen face going misty and slack—secreting themselves into his consciousness; he couldn't bear them; he craved the blackouts.

His trembling hands fumbled with his shoes. He ran his hands through his greasy hair to comb it back. He buttoned his shirt and found his car keys jammed in one of his pockets.

On his way out the door he took one last glance at the wreck that was his apartment. His eyes were drawn to the skewed coffee table and the shaky scribbling he'd apparently carved there in the wood: *Harlan was here.*

Was he? Was he really?

* * *

"Holy shit. Who the fuck is that?"

His ex-wife said something, but her words were incomprehensible through her blubbering tears.

The scene was from a nightmare. The man's body lay spread-eagle on his back, his face an inexplicable dark concave stain. The jewelry tree was a gore-hung weapon out of hell.

Blood spattered the carpet and the surrounding furniture; the dolls in the nearby hutch stare in ghastly accusation at a splattered line of gore cutting across their glass enclosure. His ex-wife was standing in the entryway between the kitchen and the living room, her face as pale as those of her dolls, her frail over-scrubbed hands wringing each other raw; her hair hung limply about her face, still wet from a recent shower. His son, Jake, was sitting on the stairs wearing an expression of stunned bewilderment.

"I said: who is that?"

"That's her boyfriend — Trevor," Jake answered.

"Boyfriend?"

Jess said something and came to him and he held her tight and let her cry into the crook of his shoulder.

"How did this happen?" Harlan tried gently.

He waited for Jess to gain control of herself, and, after a time, she managed, "He was going to take Jake. He was going to kill me and then take Jake away."

"Who is he?"

"Trevor," Jake interjected, "her boyfriend."

"Let your mom talk, Jake. Where did you meet this guy?"

She wiped her nose on his shirt. "In college."

"What? In college? Who is this guy?"

"Trevor. Don't you remember? From college."

"Your ex-boyfriend Trevor? That freak you went out with a few times when we were broken up? Trevor Greene? *That* Trevor?"

"Yes."

Harlan looked at the place where Trevor's face used to be. "Good God. What the fuck happened?"

"Mom killed him," Jake said.

"He tried to kidnap Jake."

Harlan's head spun. "Why the fuck would he want to do that?"

"I..." Jess said, "don't know."

"Well, shit. We have to call the cops," Harlan said.

Jess clutched him tight. "No. Please."

Harlan gripped her by the shoulders and pushed her to arms length; she cringed. "Jess." Harlan looked her in the eyes. "We have to. We don't have a choice."

Jess's eyes are tormented, unfocused watery globs. She didn't say anything.

Harlan let her go. "We just have to cover him up, is all," he said.

"I'll get a blanket," Jake said, and disappeared up the stairs.

A moment later, Jake reappeared, coming down

the stairs with an old quilt from the upstairs linen closet. "Here," he said, passing it to Harlan.

Harlan tried not to look too closely at the dead man as he approached, the old quilt raised open between both of his hands. He stepped up to the carcass, preparing to drape the quilt over the body.

One of the dead man's hands reached out and grabbed his ankle.

Harlan gasped and stepped back. The hand lay limply on the blood-soaked carpet.

His ankle felt cold from its touch, but he must have imagined it, he told himself. He must have been a little more shaken up than he realized. Jake wasn't looking and Jess had turned away.

He flung the quilt up and let it settle down over the dead man's body like a parachute. Blood began to seep through where the cloth clung to the man's face almost immediately.

Harlan stepped back. "Okay," he said.

Jess had disappeared; she was in the kitchen looking for a drink, Harlan figured.

Jake had returned to his spot on the stairs.

"Okay," Harlan said again, "I better call up the police now," and he turned towards the kitchen.

"Hey, Dad," Jake said.

Harlan turned.

"You're my real dad, right?"

"Of course I am."

"Good."

Harlan balanced the receiver of the kitchen phone between his shoulder and ear and dialed the police. His ankle was cold and his foot was numb. He could feel the cold crawling up his leg like bad circulation.

THIRTEEN

*Fire — he'd learned once he'd really seen it in action —
is everywhere and all around him. It mesmerizes and it
eats, and it lives only as long as it continues to find an
ample supply of things to consume.*

*And it's everywhere and he knows he started it. The
familiar guilt tugs at the back of his mind, but he's distracted. He can't be concerned with that right now.*

*In the center of the grove of trees, in a clear spot, he
stands, unafraid, simply basking in the heat and the moment. He knows the Melting Man is somewhere close,
wishing to lead him somewhere he doesn't want to go, but
right now, at this very moment, he feels just fine. He enjoys the tickling of the sweat running down his back and
the flushing heat in his face. He stands and waits and perhaps this time he'll awaken before he's forced to turn and*

see that face, before he begins to feel the fear over what he's done, of the fire he's started.

And there is a stirring before him, something different, something new; there is something in the air, faintly writhing and turning. He can hardly see what it is. And he feels something in himself, a sensation he's not felt before; a smoldering urgency – and he holds back, wary of his own body. Still, there is a need within him, an unarguable pull towards something he doesn't understand. The stirring is right there, gentle curves like smoke, bent before him, easing him forward, inviting his need towards satiation.

He is drawn in, warm and wet. It's strange, and it's slick. And there is a rumbling, almost immediately, a tightening below, and then something is happening to him. He gasps, and forgets all else in the world as pure sensation takes over everything and jolts of feeling rush through him.

And, before he awakens into the middle of the night and discovers the cold and sticky blotches of moisture on his stomach, he sees the Melting Man in the flaming bushes, shrugging and shaking his head. The stirring abstract transparency slinks away, fading into the flames.

*   *   *

That dream felt very far from him now — its confusions; its pleasures; concealed from his waking self — as the day had progressed and he'd seen the strange thing in the drainage pipe. His parents had kept him out of school, thinking he'd be traumatized by what he'd seen and a couple days "of rest" would be good for him, but they were wrong. Trevor was dead and he didn't care. Good riddance. So, he'd spent his time wandering the creek, aimlessly — all the other kids locked up at school, including Jesse — feeling alone and forgotten. The day had been cloudy and he stayed out as long as he could, avoiding the tension and pretense of his parents as they sorted out the whole messy business with the police.

Something, which had been lurking in the dark, had shuffled towards him. Besides that, the day had been pretty normal, even boring.

Jake picked a flat rock from the ground and sent it spinning and skidding across the flat bed of the ditch, splashing twice in the shallow rivulets of water before lying still. The ditch was nearly dry; what little water remained crept sluggishly downstream. Jake's sneakers padded over the sand. He approached a small sunken patch of ground where the creek collected and lay still, water reeds and grasses grew halfheartedly from the tiny swamp, grasping feebly from the mire. He came to the edge of this swampy patch and stopped. He knew you could sometimes catch small frogs here. Once, he'd caught a tadpole from one of the standing pools in a jar and put it in a blue plastic wading pool in the backyard at home. That summer he'd watched the tadpole grow legs and eventually one of those flat frog heads and one day it'd been gone, jumped right out of the water and bounded off to its life on land.

Jake waded into the water and immediately spotted a small frog sitting on a grassy patch towards the center of the swamp. Jake liked to catch the frogs, if he could. He liked to hold them cupped between his hands and watch their throats flutter, just to see them up close. Then, he'd let them go.

Maybe he'd catch one and keep it in a jar this time, he thought. That way it'd be safe from predators and wouldn't be eaten by a bird or stomped on by some kid.

He crept forward carefully. The frog didn't move.

*   *   *

He'd passed by the drainage pipe a million times; he'd always been fascinated by it. It opened beneath the dirt bike path that led to school, and the water, which trickled from it constantly, had created a patch of rocks grown a luminescent green with algae. Its concrete opening was like a gaping cave entrance. It was dank, and dark, and fascinating; it smelled of deep subterranean life and mystery. Kids sometimes dared each other to go inside, to see who had the guts to go in the deepest, but it was too dark to go far. Jake had never gone beyond the opening, but he'd heard about a kid once — whose name changed depending on who told the story — many years ago, who'd taken a flashlight and gone inside, never to be heard from again; which was total bullshit, of course. It was just a drainage pipe, spanning from one side of the neighborhood to the other, but it was easy to imagine some sort of mutant sewage man living down there, feeding on the rats and the occasional adventurous kid.

This morning, Jake had been walking slowly along the creek bed, when he'd come to the drainage pipe. He'd made his way up the slippery rocks — marveling, for a moment, at a small clear pool filled with smooth pebbles that stood beneath one of the larger rocks — and peered into the dark tunnel.

Just out of the reach of the light, something moved. He hoisted himself up and stood in the opening of the tunnel; he was careful to place his feet apart to either side of the tunnel in order to avoid the algae-slicked center. The thing in the tunnel splashed lightly in the water. He took a couple of steps into the shade of the tunnel. He could feel the temperature drop as he took another couple of steps forward, the darkness closing over him like a veil. He heard the thing move again. It was right in front of him, but he couldn't see it very well. He bent down to get a better look.

It took him a moment to realize what he was looking at and how close he'd put his face to it.

It had a face, a human face, molded onto a molten glob of red flesh. It groaned, and one eye opened and slid upwards to look in his direction.

He pulled himself away in utter disgust, his entire body shaking. He turned to flee and one of his feet was stuck in it, like sucking tar; he yanked, freed himself and ran, slipping and sliding in the confines of the tunnel. He heard the thing shuffle after him. He nearly fell upon the jagged rocks outside the tunnel, but managed to keep his feet, and ran away down the creek.

Later, he remembered something his dad had told him a couple of times: "You have one hell of an imagination, Jake. Don't ever lose that." In this case, he thought his dad was probably right and he'd been imagining things — just like his dreams were so real — but he didn't know what his dad was talking about: he didn't want to have an imagination if it was going to be like this.

* * *

Jake lunged forward, snatching the frog with his hands. He didn't see it jump away; he must have caught it. Carefully, cupping both hands together to keep the frog from escaping, he opened his hands a crack and peered inside.

There was something in there, but it wasn't moving.

He opened his hands: the frog's body was half-smeared across his palm; only its little head remained recognizable, open mouth gaping, turned upwards in a frozen cry.

He jerked his hand to his pants, wiping the slimy remains on his jeans; he waved his hands around in disgust, clenched his jaw, and shook himself to be rid of that mushy-rotten feeling.

He looked around. A clammy shudder ran through him. He is up to his ankles in murky water and they are everywhere; he is surrounded by them.

The water is stagnant with floating amphibian carcasses. They stare sightlessly at him from the rocks and grassy patches. They lie about on their backs; shriveled; decomposing. From a strand of leaning grass inches from him, a decomposing glob seems to reach for him, bending in the wind, a tiny three-toed limb jutting outward in a crusty greeting, froggy mouth open in a silent, gurgling wail.

He screamed, and wrenched his body forward, flinging himself from the swamp, arms upraised like a flailing chimp. He broke into a run, overcome with disgust, heading down the creek bed and didn't stop until he got to Sherwood Forest.

There, he tried to catch his breath.

It sucks having a good imagination, he thought. *It really fucking sucks.*

FOURTEEN

Harlan called the police and the police came out to the house and Jess watched the exchange from a numbed distance and felt something like grief, watching the first officer cringe at the sight of the scene, holding his hand over his nose and mouth, as if to protect himself from inhaling the corruption of the splayed body. Then, the masks and rubber gloves came out and the small band of police officers began to snap pictures, and collect their samples in little plastic baggies, and Jess is standing right there as one of the officers produces a notepad from his jacket pocket and begins to ask questions and Harlan answers them, but she doesn't catch a single word and just nods.

"Ma'am?"

"Mm."

"You want to tell me your side of the story? I understand this man attacked you. Is that right?"

Harlan nudged her and she shook her head, trying to clear it. "Uh. Yes. Of course, of course. My side of the story."

She answered the officer's questions the best she could, but her responses are hollow. It's as if someone else is answering for her, as she's sure Harlan has already tried to do. She tells them about her strange two week affair with Trevor. She tells them about him getting angry all of a sudden and attacking her and chasing her up the stairs so she had to hide in the back bedroom. She tells them about how Trevor was trying to convince Jake to go with him, how he was trying to kidnap her son.

She does *not* tell them Trevor was an ex-boyfriend from college. She does *not* tell them the things Trevor said about being Jake's father; it is simply untrue and not to be spoken of or discussed. She *does* tell them she had to defend herself; she didn't have a choice; he wouldn't stay down; he would have killed her if she hadn't.

When the officer finally lets her go, she slunk back to the kitchen and pulled a stool up to the counter. She slid the drawer open and plucked one of her little bottles from the top of the office supply junk pile. She drank it; feels nothing. Drank another one. She can hear Harlan's voice going on and on to the police officers in the other room.

Oh, Trevor, she thinks. *What the hell were you doing here?*

She downed another bottle and grimaced in disgust.

*   *   *

Pulling up to the house, parking against the curb on the street, Jess says: "It's cute. What do you think, hubby-bear?"

Harlan makes a face at the mock term of affection. "It looks big enough anyway. You think we can afford it."

"Why not? We'll convert the biggest room in the house into the nicest office you've ever seen, with one of those huge oak desks where you can spread out all your notes and write your next Great American Screenplay."

Harlan makes a huffing sound. "Yeah, right; we'll see," he says and smiles.

From the back seat, a four-year-old Jake squeals: "We'll take it!"

Jess and Harlan laugh together.

The real estate agent is waiting for them on the front porch. "Welcome, welcome," she says. "Shall we take a look at this place?" She smiles.

They follow the agent inside, Jess and Harlan side by side, Jake trailing behind, his little hand gripping a fold of Harlan's pants.

In the entryway the agent shakes their hands. "It's good to see you again," she says. "And I don't believe I've met the little one." She squats to get a better view of Jake hiding amongst his parent's legs like the trunks of trees. "Hi, I'm Caroline," she says. She stands. "Doesn't talk much does he?"

"He's a little shy," Jess says.

Harlan ruffles the hair on Jake's head. "Yeah, he's a total weirdo. We've had his head examined and the doctors tell us there's nothing we can do."

104

Jake giggles.

The real estate lady smiles warmly. "Well, okay; shall we see the house? Here, as you can see, is the living room..."

The house has four bedrooms and three bathrooms, a large kitchen, spacious dining room/living room area, an upstairs and a downstairs, and an unfinished basement. It has a lot of old blue-gray carpet, too many whitewashed walls, and an uninspiring floor plan. Still, the house is perfect and in a good neighborhood and they can afford it and Jess already knows — only half-way through the tour — they are going to buy it and be very happy living in it.

"...and the fireplace is very large for a house this size and centrally located; the previous owners used it to offset their power bill during the winter..."

Jess stops at the sliding glass door to the back yard and watches Jake running around in the grass back there, his arms out like the wings on an airplane. He needs another haircut, *she thinks to herself absently.*

"I let him out to play," Harlan says over her shoulder, coming up behind her. "He was getting restless in here with us adults." He kisses her neck and hugs her from behind.

"What do you think?" Harlan says.

"It's nice."

"You think we should get it, don't you?"

She shrugs and squeezes Harlan's hand.

"Alright," Harlan whispers in her ear. "Let's get it."

*   *   *

A few months later, there are still boxes piled in the corners, but she has arranged the living room to be as com-

fortable as possible. She hasn't bothered with the Christmas decorations this year — they're still in a box in the basement — but the pile of presents for the family is significant; they're stacked, for convenience, in lieu of a tree, beneath the television set. They add much needed color to the largely undecorated room and Jake has taken to wriggling behind the television and the wall of presents, enjoying the private conclave created there where he can play with his toys privately. And it's okay, even if she can't see exactly what he's doing, because Jessica knows he's close by and safe.

Sometimes she can hear Jake muttering to himself as she sits on the couch, folding laundry or sorting through another box of junk that needs to be unpacked, the TV on low to the afternoon talk shows, her son's toddler voice faint and shrill, as if he's having a conversation with someone. But it's okay. She knows about his imaginary friend. They call him ZimZim — the name slurred from Jake's mouth when he was only two years old — and Jake talks to him sometimes. It's only natural. He's too young to have any real friends yet. When he goes off to school he'll learn to socialize with the other kids and forget all about ZimZim.

Most of the time — the few times she's tried — she can't understand what Jake is saying anyway. He's too young, his voice still developing. She only knows of the few times she's dropped a dish to shatter on the kitchen floor, or knocked a glass of water over on the table, or stubbed her toe on one of the end tables, he's said: "ZimZim says uh-oh." And she knows it's probably just her motherly worries over Jake, but it's uncanny; she thinks she hears him say this right before she does one of these things. She knows it must be after, and her brain is playing tricks with her, but it really seems sometimes like her son knows she's going to *do something "bad" before she does it.*

On this particular day, however, she hears much more; Jake's voice rises from its usual muttering whisper and says: "No, I don't wanna see." Then, "Leave me alone!"

Jessica stands with a start, dropping the socks she's just paired to the floor. "Jake?" she calls. "Are you okay back there?" She goes to the TV and peers over it and sees Jake crouched on the floor with his head in his hands, shaking back and forth. It's strange, Jessica thinks, that pose, sitting there shaking his head (no, no, no) doesn't look right on her four-year-old son; it's a grownup action, a stressed out I've-too-much-to-do grownup thing to do. "Jake?" she says again, and her son looks up and his face softens immediately at the sight of her. "Are you okay?"

Jake raises his hands to be picked up. "Mommy," he says.

Jessica bends over the TV and lifts her son up out of his conclave. He's getting a little too heavy for this sort of thing, but he's a small boy for his age so she manages. She sets him down on the floor in front of the TV. "Are you okay, Jake?" she asks again.

"I'm okay." Then, Jake grabs the sock ball she dropped from the ground and pulls it apart. He starts twirling the separated socks, one in each hand.

"Hey," Jessica says, "I was folding those."

Jake giggles and makes a run for it across the carpeted living room.

She chases him. "Come back here," she says. "I'm going to get you."

Jake squeals delightedly at the game and Jessica forgets all about the strange things her son said a second ago as she chases him around the house.

Jake makes a break for the stairs and Harlan appears at

the top. "What's going on here?" Harlan says.

"We have a little thief on our hands," Jessica says.

"Oh, a thief, huh?" Harlan starts down the stairs. "Well, we can't allow that sort of behavior around here, can we?"

Jake squeals again and turns to run towards the kitchen.

Harlan comes down the stairs and catches Jake and they wrestle and Harlan tickles Jake and Jake giggles and giggles uncontrollably and Jessica stands over them shaking her head. "Oh, you two," she says.

*   *   *

The point was, there *were* good times; times Jessica can remember being happy, all of them being happy — herself, Harlan, and Jake. She had never really concerned herself with her son's behavior, other than having to be careful with the TV around him (he was mesmerized by it and would stare for hours entranced by the flashing images if Jessica didn't shake him and tell him to go and play outside); she was never too worried. Before long, Jake stopped talking to ZimZim and Harlan and her assumed that phase of their son's life was over. Harlan tried to write, but he only became more and more restless. They had to sell one of their cars, but it wasn't like they were completely irresponsible with their money — Jessica made sure of that. They managed to keep their house and she paid their debts down slowly. It was just, Harlan was never the same after his writing dreams fizzled out; he was depressed and distant. He made her depressed and distant; in order to stay with him

108

she had to lower herself, she never did it on purpose; she tried to cheer him up, to assure him she didn't care that he wasn't going to be a famous screenwriter, that she was happy to have him and their family and that was all that mattered (and it was true, that *was* all she really wanted), but Harlan wouldn't snap out of it; he turned to drink and drugs and she began to drink as well.

They'd been happy, for a time. But now, their family was broken. Where had it all gone wrong? What could she have done differently? Was there no fixing this apparently irreparable rift between her and Harlan? It was all such a mess.

*   *   *

The police officers told her they'd be in touch and that they hadn't been able to locate any family members of Trevor's. They told her that unless someone related to Trevor decided to press charges, they would file the case as one of self defense against domestic abuse resulting in homicide.

Jessica thanked the officers and saw them to the door.

The body was carted away, leaving only the blood-stained carpet as a reminder.

Harlan said he was going to stay over a few nights and she told him that was fine as long as he slept in the other room. Jake was out playing while all this was going on. The next few days were a blur.

FIFTEEN

An elongated arm snakes out of the television screen, snatches the little boy Denny by the head and lightning shoots from the screen. The arm shakes the boy — the boys' face slackens — and then stops. The boy begins to grin.

Denny walks stiffly across the house and to the kitchen. He slides a wicked-looking knife from its block on the counter. He holds it up, pointing the blade outwards.

"What are you doing?"

Denny turns and Denny's father is standing in the doorway.

"Give me the knife," Denny's father says.

"I don't think so, old man," Denny says, his voice a guttural growl, and lunges forward.

Denny's father tries to jump back, but the knife catches him in the leg and he stumbles. He staggers out into the living room. He kicks Denny away, but Denny jumps up and drives the knife deep into his father's side.

Denny laughs and stabs the knife. The blade glints; flashes off screen; comes up dripping blood. Denny's father lies still.

Denny goes over to the crib in the corner of the room. He drops the bloody knife in the crib next to where the baby lies. He leans over the crib and lifts the baby up into his arms. He croons to it, rocking little baby Devin back and forth.

"Put him down." Denny's mother stands in the front doorway, framed against a roiling thunderstorm.

Denny turns. "Now the bitch wants to play too."

Denny's mother steps into the house, her long black hair hanging, wet lines parallel to her face. "What do you want with my baby?" she says.

Denny grins demonically. "A prophet," he says, "to open our realm to yours."

"Give Devin to me."

"Never."

The television flashes with scenes of hellish torture. Denny steps towards it.

"Give me my baby."

The picture on the television screen is scrambled, begins to bulge and ripple. "I don't think so," the demon inside Denny says, edging closer and closer to the beckoning screen.

Denny's mother lunges forward.

Denny reaches the screen and begins to melt into it. But, before he can fully enveloped by it, an arm shoots out and grabs his ankle.

Denny's father yanks.

Little boy Denny tumbles down, his head striking the hearth of the brick fireplace with the sound of a melon bursting upon a rock.

"Noooooooo…"

Little baby Devin rolls free.

The television explodes. Fire begins to assail the curtains and then the walls of the house.

Denny's mother snatches her baby from the floor and holds him close. She goes to Denny's father.

"I'm sorry," Denny's father says.

"No. It's okay. I'm going to get you out of here," Denny's mother says.

"Go. Please. Take good care of Devin," Denny's father chokes out. "I wish I could be there for him," he gasps and dies.

Denny's mother stands. The fire in the house rages around her. She blows a kiss to her dead husband and then runs from the house. She is half way across the front yard when the house goes up in a dramatic ball of lightning and fire and she's thrown to the ground.

Denny's mother stands on the sidewalk in silhouette against the backdrop of the burning house, her tiny baby cradled in her arms. A close up shot shows her face glimmering with reflected flame, a determined scowl creasing her smooth, soot-smudged face.

The picture fades to black.

*　*　*

The New Flesh, in Harlan's opinion, was an exercise in camp and the ridiculous. He's surprised it made a splash at all in the world of horror films. He can't say, unfortunately, that it was his writing that lifted the film to a level beyond forgettable B-rate trash, but the cinematography and the mis-en-scene work of Mark Sutterburg and Susan Goya, respectively, that made the film a delight to watch. He's proud to have been a part of *The New Flesh* and it was a thrilling experience to watch his vision come to life.

It's strange, where ideas come from. His inspiration for *The New Flesh* had come from watching how his son behaved around the TV. He'd watched Jake, at a very early age, become completely enthralled when the TV was on (like any boy his age, of course) and that had given him the idea for his screenplay. He'd even borrowed the name of his son's imaginary friend—changing it only slightly from ZimZim to ZigZig—as a name for the demon in the film whom uses the television as a means of access to our world from his alternate dimension and eventually possesses Denny.

It has been a while since he's thought about his film—he used to think about it a lot—but these past couple of days, sulking around the old house—his ex-wife avoiding him, keeping mostly to herself, not even speaking to him—he's had time to reminisce. His movie reminds him of better times. Even the family in the movie (based on his own, he has to admit), whose domestic arguments between Denny's mother and father brim towards violence, don't seem so bad now, not compared with divorce and estrangement, with this grating silence between him and Jess.

*   *   *

After three days of hanging around the old house, Jess not speaking to him and Jake always playing outside somewhere so that he hardly ever sees him, he decides to return to his apartment. He hasn't had a drop of alcohol during this time. He feels okay — better, really.

The first thing he does when he gets to his apartment — peeling the door open, immediately assaulted by the reek of alcohol, mildew, cigarettes, and a sink of dirty dishes filled with flotsam that makes his nose and eyes burn — is to clean the place up. It takes him several hours. He picks up everything, vacuums and shampoos the carpet, wipes things down, and puts all of his movies back in their proper places and order. When he's finally finished, and is able to stand back and see the results of his efforts, he feels better than he has in a long while. He almost feels good. He feels like life can return to normal.

*　　*　　*

He slumped into the couch. He sipped his Coke and leaned his head back, letting his eyes slide shut.

For a moment, an image rises in his mind. He can see Trevor's body, splayed out on the floor as if for scientific research, and where his face used to be: an opening of dark and squiggling red. And standing over the body, looking down at him, is Grace. She smiles, and the masked men step forward to choke her.

Harlan jerked, splashing Coke across the couch and the seat of his pants. He pushed these thoughts, these images, out of his head. *Not now*, he thought. *I'll deal with these things later, when I'm ready. Just, not now. Not yet.*

He looked at his coffee table. The only thing he couldn't return to normal was the fucking coffee table. He'd need a new one. For now, he'd spread a few drink coasters over the scratches. What in the world had he been thinking, carving *"Harlan was here"* into the finished wood?

Harlan's right here, right now, he thinks. No more binge drinking nightmare blackouts. He just needed to get out of his place for a while. It's good to be back.

A knock at the door: three slow taps. *Tap. Tap. Tap.*

Harlan froze in mid-stride, on his way to the kitchen to get himself another Coke. For a second, it all came crashing back to him: the grief, the self-loathing—the frightened voice always at the back of his mind near panic. In that moment he wanted a drink more than he'd ever wanted anything in his life and he'd do anything to get one; the yearning was almost physical, a dawning pain in his chest. If it's another video, he thought he was going to scream.

Harlan took a deep breath. It was probably nothing, he assured himself. He stepped to the door; put his hand on the doorknob.

He swung the door open. His breath caught in his throat.

For a moment it felt like he'd stepped into another of his strange hangover dreams; he couldn't believe his eyes.

"Harlan, darling. Did you miss me?"

He couldn't speak. He couldn't think what to say.

"Oh, darling, are you alright?"

"How long has it been?" he managed lamely.

"Just a few days. May I come in?"

"Sure, of course."

Grace stepped into his apartment and Harlan embraces her and they hold each other for a couple of minutes and it felt good and then she kissed him and her lips are a little cold but he kissed her back to warm them up and he realized for the first time that he might have real feelings for her and that he missed her more than he thought.

Harlan invited her to have a seat on the couch and he has so many questions, but before he gets a chance she's on top of him and pulling his pants down and he's in her mouth and it feels so good to have human contact, to have Grace back with him.

When they were done, Grace got up and sauntered towards the kitchen, her naked backside swinging suggestively as she went, leaving Harlan panting on the couch. "How about a drink?" she said.

Harlan felt really good. "Well, alright. Why the hell not?"

The sound of ice clinking into glasses came from the kitchen.

"I saw your video," Harlan said.

"Oh, yeah?"

"It was a little freaky. I thought, maybe…What happened to you?"

Grace returned with two glasses of scotch on the rocks; she smiled that canted smile of hers. "It was wild," she said. "It was a really wild time."

SIXTEEN

The nightmare came to him every night now. Crouching in the grass, he'd light the match, drop it, and stare. He'd enjoy watching the flames dance, and burn, and grow. He'd feel the heat on his face and the trickles of sweat. He'd feel powerful and alive.

Then, he'd be standing in the forest, wreathed in flame, watching the world burn because of him. He'd feel the loss of control, and the despair. He'd watch the horses kicking their feet and running from the flames. And his dream would shift and get weird and he'd be talking with the Melting Man even though he didn't want to. The Melting Man would tell him things, ask him to go with him, then fade and contort.

He'd wake, bolting upright to a sitting position, with his skin feeling hot, and flushed, and bubbly, with a scream twisted and caught in his throat but never released. He'd wake into the guilt. He'd nearly burned the whole goddamn neighborhood down. He worried he might do it again, that there was something inside of him that yearned for the destruction. Someday, he might not be able to hold back.

* * *

At least his mom was letting him go back to school now. The past few days had been lonely and surreal. Even though he didn't really like going to school, there were still things to keep him occupied and Jesse to talk to. Time had passed like the lethargic last days of summer vacation, where he didn't want to start the new school year, but, at the same time, didn't know what to do with himself. He couldn't be at the house—it was awful being around his mom, whose moping about just made everything that much worse; his dad not much better—so all he could do was wander about by himself. He wandered about the neighborhood, and down the drainage creek, and hung out in Sherwood Forest, but never felt inspired—as he often had been—to plan and build his next tree house, or fort, or collect things for his next game with Jesse. At times he'd been so bored he'd simply sat down somewhere—in a sandy crook or against the side of a tree—and dozed. And he must have slept, because his dreams were vivid.

One of those days, plodding along in the sand of the creek bed as usual, he'd seen a couple of older boys in the distance, crouched over something. They looked down at whatever it was, their heads hunched. One of them kicked at it. As he stood there watching them, the kids stopped for a second, bringing their heads up, and they were much older than Jake had at first thought: wrinkles twisted their mouths and their coats were torn and they had mud streaks on their cheeks. Their eyes slid in his direction and stared.

Jake turned, and hurried on his way.

Another time, he lifted his head to discover a dog—some sort of brindle mutt—sniffing at his sneakers. When he brought his hand out for the dog to sniff, the animal quickly backed away, its blond-spotted hackles rising and quivering. Jake watched the dog stop a little ways away, lifting its head to sniff at the air. The dog glanced at him one last time with eyes that seemed intelligent and knowing, and broke into a trot, streaking down the open creek.

Jake looked out across the sand and, out of the corner of his eye, saw something long and spindly rise out of the dogs back, make a motion in the air, and by the time Jake had turned his head to get a better look, the mutt was gone. The animal was nowhere to be seen.

He must have slept, and it was like his dad said: he had an imagination and he used it (even though it felt, sometimes, more like *it* used *him*).

At one point he'd seen a little girl with a stick playing by the sidewalk as he walked by. She'd looked at him shyly and returned to her drawings in the dirt. Just as Jake had been about to turn the corner on to the next block, he'd heard the girl shriek, and he'd turned to see a cluster of raccoons (at least, that's what he thought they were; it was hard to tell from this distance) surrounding the little girl. He watched the raccoons pounce, and the girl disappeared beneath the furry squirming creatures.

If he'd thought what he was seeing was real, if there'd been anything he could do, he would have run back to try and help, but it couldn't be real. He shook his head—no, it couldn't—and continued on his way.

On his walk back, on that first day he'd been allowed to return to school, he came across the spot where the little girl had been. There were no scuff marks, no sign of a struggle, like he knew there wouldn't be. It was a spot of dirt surrounded by weeds. Kids played around here all the time. There was only a circle drawn in the dirt, or most of one; it was a few inches from being full, as if someone had been distracted from its completion. There were numerous footprints and a couple of discarded bottles. Looking around, just out of curiosity, a little ways from the circle, behind a small tangle of dried leaves in the brush, there was something else drawn in the dirt. It was difficult to make out, the top layer of loose sand having scattered in the breeze; he had to lean down close to read it. *"Fathers kill,"* it read.

On his way back home he thought he saw another of Mrs. Marlow's gnomes wink at him. But, of course, it was just an illusion—the sun twinkling off the pale plastic—like that finger that's always pointing at you and those eyes that always follow you on that ugly poster of Uncle Sam, the one hanging on the wall in his classroom at school: "a piece of history," his teacher called it. There were no inappropriately arranged gnomes this time—Mrs. Marlow must have discovered those from earlier and put them back where they belonged—but there did seem to be an awful lot of the little plastic men. Mrs. Marlow had been busy. There was no longer space for all of them to lurk in the flowerbeds and beneath the trees; some were staked right out in the open, smiling those faint I'm-so-high little smiles.

Coming up to Old Man Greene's house, he noticed there were two patches of upturned soil now corroding the perfection of Greene's lawn. "That sucks," Jake said to himself. As he followed the sidewalk around the yard, he was alone on the street. He heard a door slam. He turned his head and Old Man Greene was running across his lawn in a bathrobe and slippers, brandishing a shovel, coming straight towards him.

"Get off my lawn," Greene yelled. "Get off it, you little punk!"

Jake stopped; stood his ground. "I'm walking around Mr. Greene. I always do. I'm Jake. My dad's Harlan Bowden."

Greene stood at the edge of his lawn, the shovel held parallel to the ground in both hands, looking down at Jake with red-rimmed eyes brimming with mistrust. "Bowden's boy, huh? What are you doing here?"

"Just walking back from school, Mr. Greene."

Old Man Greene's slippers were caked with mud and streaks of greenish-yellow grass stains. His robe was dirty, torn in one place so that it hung open at the chest.

Greene grunted. "Well, alright. Get on home then."

"Have a good day, Mr. Greene," Jake called as he headed on his way, walking fast.

"Yeah, right. Just look what those bastard kids

made me do to my lawn."

Jake made it around the next corner, his heart beating a little too fast, and hurried all the rest of the way home.

*   *   *

He let himself into the house. He passed through the living room, passed his mom slouched on the couch watching TV.

"Hi, Jake."

"Hi, Mom."

He jumped up the stairs and down the hall to his room. He closed the door firmly after him.

He tossed his backpack on the floor, flopped on the bed, and flipped the TV on using the remote. He sat up, kicked his sneakers off, and looked around his room. He stood up, went to his dresser. Buried in the top drawer, at the bottom of his balled up collection of socks and underwear, he fished out a small silver lighter he'd found the other day.

He just wanted to hold it. He didn't light it. He knew he shouldn't have picked it up, but it was just lying there on the sidewalk.

He'd also found a couple of matchbooks.

After a while, he put the lighter back and turned his attention to the glowing television screen.

SEVENTEEN

Jessica awoke in the middle of the night, sick to her stomach. She dropped out of bed, clutching her midsection, and staggered to the bathroom. Her knees hit the cold tile of the floor and she retched in the dark into the open maw of the toilet. Her clammy hands grasped the cold porcelain; straggles of her hair curled on the surface of the pale water. She retched again and hot, alcoholic bile rose and poured from between her lips. She gasped, and her vomit splashed and steamed in the toilet.

When her stomach's roiling had subsided, she fell back on the floor, leaning against the wall. She groaned.

Tap-tap-tap. "Mom? Are you okay?"

Jess jumped, her heart lurching to life in her chest. "Fine, Jake," she said. "I'm fine."

"Okay..." Her son sounded like he wanted to say more, but he didn't and Jess heard his footsteps padding away down the hallway. After a second, she heard the door to his bedroom close lightly.

"Shit," Jess mumbled.

She stood, gaining herself on wobbly legs. Her head throbbed. Her throat felt raw and cut up, like she'd tried to swallow a wad of that pink fiberglass insulation that grew in the walls. She was also a little sore between the legs.

She froze — suddenly — her eyes darting about the nearly light-less room. She braced herself against the towel rack. Had she had her period this month? How many days had it been? Too many, she already knew, even without looking at the calendar. She knew because she'd used the last of her tampons the month before and knew she'd need to restock her supply for the next month — this month.

She groaned again. It was the middle of the night; she'd worry about it in the morning.

Jess shuffled back to bed, folded herself beneath the blankets, gingerly lowered her head to the pillow and — after a while — passed into unconsciousness.

*   *   *

The next day was Saturday. Jake didn't have school. She sat at the dining room table with a bagel, absently smearing cream cheese over it with a tiny butter knife. Jake sat across from her and she could feel him watching her — taking quick stabbing glances at her over his bowl of colorful cereal — but she pretended not to notice. She took a couple of aspirin with a sip of her orange juice (you could hardly call it a screwdriver, it had only the tiniest splash of vodka in it), and took a bite of her bagel; even with all the cream cheese she was using the bagel soon became a dry gelatinous lump in her mouth, but she choked it down. She took another sip of orange juice and took a cigarette from her pack sitting next to the tub of cream cheese. She snapped her lighter to life and she could feel Jake tense. That boy was too jumpy these days, she thought. He was probably trauma-tized from that whole messy Trevor business; who wouldn't be? She was freaked out herself.

"So," she tried, "what are you going to do today, Jake?"

Jake watched his cereal. "I don't know."

"You should go out and play; have some fun; it's Saturday. Maybe you can call up your friend Jesse and see what he's doing?"

"Yeah. Maybe."

She dragged deeply on her cigarette and talked through the exhaled smoke. "I have to go to the store this morning and get a few things. I'll be back before lunch time."

Jake lifted his head and looked at her hopefully. "Can I go with you?"

"You want to go with me? I'm only going to the grocery store. I don't want you to be bored."

Jake nodded. "Yeah, okay."

"I'll be back before you know it."

"Sure. Okay."

*   *   *

125

Jess pulled one of the little white and pink boxes off the shelf and dropped it into her shopping basket. She also picked up some other things: Cokes, a loaf of bread, a bottle of mouthwash. She'd normally get this stuff from the grocery store instead of the drug store, but she was afraid the checkout clerk might say something if all she got was the pregnancy test, especially if it was Tony, the same clerk she purchased her little bottles of vodka from. "Congratulations," Tony might say, "I didn't know you were trying." Or worse: "That's what drinking will get you. Am I right?" Or some other such nonsense.

Of course, if she really were pregnant, she was going to have to stop drinking. That was part of it. It was just, this voice in the back of her mind kept nagging her, telling her she couldn't stop, not right now; drinking was all she had. And what if she wasn't able to quit this time? What if she was an alcoholic now and she'd get sick and get the shakes if she stopped suddenly, like her Great Uncle Rupert? But that was ridiculous. She'd stopped before, even forgotten to drink and skipped a couple of days here and there. She only drank now because she was sad about her divorce, and traumatized from Trevor nearly choking her to death. And — it slipped into her mind before she could stop it — she was bored. Perhaps this new baby was exactly what she needed to find meaning in her life again. Jake practically took care of himself now; he didn't need her anymore. A new baby would be a new beginning. She'd assure Harlan it wasn't Trevor's baby, that she'd been with another man and he was a good guy, but not right for her and he'd moved away. Harlan wouldn't like it if it were Trevor's baby.

Harlan wouldn't like it being any other man's baby, but there was no other way. Harlan needed to believe this baby was a happy accident from someone he didn't know and was okay with. Maybe—another thought slipped into her mind before she could push it away—the new baby might even help them to reconcile their marriage. A new start, for their whole family. She'd always hoped, maybe, there would be a way for them to get along again—for Jake's sake, of course. But that was a fool's hope and she knew it.

But she'd been letting her mind wander; she didn't even know if she was pregnant or not yet. She was holding a bottle of shampoo; she dropped it in her basket and approached the checkout counter.

The checkout person was a woman and she rung Jess's items up with a gloomy lack of comment, which Jess was grateful for.

Over the woman's shoulders, Jess could see the glass cabinet and shelves with all the cigarettes and liquor bottles. She considered getting a few more little bottles of vodka, or maybe just a bottle of peppermint schnapps, something light and unobtrusive.

Looking at the cigarettes, she realized she'd have to quit smoking as well.

The checkout clerk looked up at her with glazed, disinterested eyes. "$42.58," she said.

Jess paid the bill with her debit card and left.

*   *   *

When she got back to the house, she called Jake's name, but he was nowhere to be found. He must be out playing, she thought.

She went to the kitchen and unloaded her purchases slowly and carefully. She wanted a drink, but she wouldn't have one. She placed the box of home pregnancy tests on the counter and looked at it. She turned it over and read the back of the box.

"Okay, here we go," she said to herself.

She carefully tore open one end of the box, slid one of the tests wrapped in plastic out, and took it with her to the bathroom.

When she was done, she left the little plastic stick on the counter in the bathroom and came back to the kitchen. She took a glass from the cabinet. She filled the glass with water from the tap. She drank. Then she forced herself to drink a little more.

She returned to the bathroom and knew before she'd even crossed the tiled bathroom floor to the counter what the test would say. She picked up the stick and held it close to her face.

Positive. Yes, she was pregnant.

EIGHTEEN

"Why didn't you call?" Harlan was angry; he couldn't help himself.

"I wasn't allowed. They're very secretive over there, you know."

"You weren't allowed? But I've been sitting on my ass in my apartment for a week without any idea what happened to you. Then I got your video and I thought you were dead. I called the police. Did you know that? I even called the fucking police?"

Grace sipped her martini, met his gaze over the glass. "Don't make a scene, Harlan," she said calmly.

Harlan slammed his fist on the table, harder than he meant to, the silverware and dishes rattling—he didn't care if this was a nice restaurant. "God damn it. I thought you were dead. Doesn't that mean anything to you?"

Grace shook her head, putting her glass to rest back on the table. "Of course it does, but I didn't have a choice in the matter. You must understand that."

Harlan slouched in his chair, crossing his arms. "Fine, I guess. Well, what happened then?"

"I found the guys who make those videos and I wanted to be in one of them so I was." Grace shrugged. "It was not a very impressive place, really. A small operation."

"So you found the studio, then?"

"Yes. It's closer than you think."

Harlan leaned forward. "What were they like?"

"Oh, they were nice. Polite. You should put their videos on your website. I'm sure you could sell them."

"You talked business?"

"A little."

"That video...it was so real. Are you sure you're okay?"

Grace laughed. "Of course. Of course."

"That bruise on your neck is real, I know that much."

Grace's hands shot up to the scarf she was wearing. "Not here, Harlan. Please."

"So?" Harlan said. "That's it?"

"That's it."

Harlan sat back in his chair, taking the cloth napkin from his lap and placing it on the table. "I was so worried, I...it was weird. I'm, I guess...I'm just happy to have you back. I'm glad you're okay."

Grace flashed him her sarcastic smile. "Me too," she said. "Me too."

*   *   *

"You know why I like you, Harlan?" Grace said when they got back to his apartment.

"Why's that?"

"I like that I can be myself around you." Grace walked to the middle of the living room, turned, and casually brushed the straps on her dress over the sides of her shoulders. She wiggled slightly and her dress fluttered down to her feet. She was standing there in nothing but her panties and heels, her dress pooled at her feet, her hip cocked slightly to one side.

Harlan gaped. He was always caught off guard by Grace's spontaneous sexual hungers. He could feel himself stiffening uncomfortably in his slacks.

"I want you to hit me, Harlan."

"Hit you?"

Grace approached him slowly. "Yes. I want you to hit me. Be rough with me. Do whatever you want. I'm yours."

Grace stood close to him, her face inches from his; her breath tinged with the garlic-heavy Italian food they'd eaten at the restaurant and something else, but already he didn't care. He could feel her hands on him, unzipping his pants, pulling him out, stroking him gently.

He moaned as she knelt and drew him into her mouth. She sucked him down her throat, all the way to the base.

Grace released him and stood. They kissed and he slipped a hand up to fondle her breast, running his fingers lightly over her cold and erect nipple. She took a step back and their eyes met for a second.

She slapped him hard across the face.

Harlan shrieked and pulled back, stunned. "What the fuck…" he heard himself saying. He felt distant, like it wasn't real. A cold, tingling sensation crept up his body, from the base of his leg, up through him.

"You bitch," his mouth said, and his fingers clutched tightly into a fist.

Grace stood, never flinching, as his fist came up and around in a wide arc. His knuckles connected with the side of her face and Grace went down. She looked up at him on hands and knees from the floor, her eyes smoldering pools of black.

He kicked her and she fell sprawling onto her back. He threw his pants down and kicked the wad with his pants and shoes off to the side. He tore his shirt free.

"Is this what you want," he was saying. "Is this what you fucking want?"

Grace writhed and moaned on the floor.

He ripped her panties from her hips to reveal the pink flesh beneath.

He fell on top of her, a growl in the back of his throat, and blacked out.

*   *   *

The next thing he's aware of, he is straddling Grace on the bed in the bedroom and she is saying, "Yes, you can. You can choke me all you want. It's okay now. I'm yours."

And, to his growing horror, his hands are already around Grace's neck and he can feel his muscles tightening, constricting the air from her throat.

Grace sputters. Her face becomes pale and faded. Her eyes roll back in their sockets.

"Stop this," he screams. "Stop right now. Stop!"

Grace's body begins to shudder beneath him. Her eyes are complete whites. A gurgling comes from her mouth; saliva glistens on her colorless lips, slides down her cheek.

And he's inside her. He can feel himself thrusting and thrusting, picking up speed. He can feel the familiar tightening in his balls, preparing to release.

Stop! He wills himself to stop. He can't. It's too late. He's not in control of himself. *Please stop!*

He comes. He can hardly feel it. The pleasure is gone, his muscles spasm, and it feels like it goes on forever and he just wants it to stop, pump after pump.

He pulls out and takes his hands from Grace's throat and puts them on her shoulder and shakes her. Grace is pale, so pale. She doesn't move.

"Please wake up," he says. "Please wake up."

He shakes her and she flops around. He bends down, putting his ear to her mouth; he can't feel her breath; the air feels cold and stale around her.

He falls back on his knees, his hands trembling before him, staring at Grace's motionless body. Her entire neck is a swollen purple, bulging outward in places, inflamed, like some sort of infected tattoo.

"Oh, fuck."

He drops his face into his hands and begins to sob; he can't help himself. He can't believe this. What is happening to him?

He cries, and he doesn't know how much time passes.

"My God, Harlan. That was good."

Harlan jumps to his feet, a yelp escaping him. He backs off a couple of steps.

Grace's eyes are open and looking at him.

"I haven't had a fuck like that in years," Grace says, then her face screws up, looking confused. "Right? Years...yes, I think that's right. It's hard to remember now. It's all muddled up in my head."

Harlan falls to his knees beside the bed. "You're okay. Really? Are you okay?" He reaches his hands out to touch her, gingerly, testing her solidity. Some of the color has returned to her face, but she is still very pale.

"I'm fine, darling. I'm great, in fact. Don't worry about me. I told you already I like it rough. You worry too much."

"Yeah, but..."

"Stop it, Harlan. And fetch me a tissue, would you? Your semen is getting all over the sheets."

NINETEEN

"How many did you get? I lost count," Jesse said.

"Hang on. Let me try again," Jake said.

The two of them sit side by side on the crumbling rock wall surrounding Mrs. Marlow's house. They're trying to count the number of gnomes, but it's proving more difficult to spot them all in the overgrown yard than they originally thought.

"I got thirty-four," Jake said.

"No way. There's more than that."

While Jesse resumed the count, a memory came to the surface of Jake's mind. It's strange, Jake thought, the things you remember and those you don't. How can anyone be sure what's really happened and what hasn't, what's real and what isn't?

*   *   *

He is with his dad and his dad is great; his dad is smiling and his dad is happy. He loves his dad. He adores him.

They are standing in a field somewhere; Jake doesn't know where exactly. The wind rustles through the grass and he can see it in the distance, the brown and yellow ripples threading across the hills like water. There is a small farmhouse over the next hill, but his dad says it's abandoned.

"Can you see them, Jake? Can you count how many there are?" his dad says.

"Yeah. Thirty-four."

His dad laughs. "You're just guessing. You didn't even try to count them." His dad points to the far off power line and the flock of tiny black birds roosting there. "See, if you close one eye and stare really hard, you can count them. Let's start from the left and work our way over."

His dad says the birds are crows. His dad says they don't get zapped because they're only touching one of the wires. Electrocuted. He says they sleep like that, in that funny way, perched on the wires.

His dad takes a knee next to him and holds Jake's hand out to point at the birds. "Okay," he says. One...two... three..."

"There's lots, huh, Daddy?"

"There sure are. Don't lose count. Twelve...thirteen... fourteen..."

Together they count the birds and Jake can't help but to sneak little glances at his dad's concentrating face. He already knows how many there are. His dad is being silly.

"Thirty-four...and thirty-five. Wow, Jake. Good job. You were really close. You have a really good eye!"

He looks at his dad, shakes his head. "No. There are thirty-four."

"How do you know?"

"ZimZim told me, Daddy." He rolls his eyes. "Duh."

His dad laughs. "Oh, of course. I forgot about ZimZim. Well, you want to count them again?"

"Okay."

His dad counts again.

"You're right. I count thirty-four this time. Maybe one flew away."

"Yeah," Jake says, "maybe."

His dad scowls and that means his dad's not happy and he doesn't want to make his dad to not be happy.

And that's the part he remembers most about that moment: the lines on his dad's forehead, wrinkling and deepening in a subtle downward slope.

*   *   *

The other time he can remember seeing his dad scowl like that had been later — a year, perhaps six months later.

In the living room they'd been roughhousing. He was zigging and zagging, jumping in to strike his dad on the leg with the television remote. His dad was growling and had puffed himself up like King Kong, his arms out at his sides like the massive and muscular ape.

His dad attacked and Jake let himself be caught and they were on the carpeted floor and he was giggling and his dad had pulled up his shirt and was tickling his exposed belly and he was giggling and giggling and couldn't stop.

These moments, he remembers fondly.

That same day, his dad is holding him at arm's length, one each of his dad's large, hot hands on his shoulders, his dad's eyes looking into his, searching.

"Jake," his dad says, "You're too old for this. ZimZim

is imaginary. He's your imaginary friend. He's not real."

Jake looks at his dad. His dad is being silly again. He blinks.

"You understand that right, Jake?"

Jake continues to look at his dad. After a moment or two, he says, "ZimZim told me you'd say that."

His dad flinches.

Then, something happens to his dad that he never forgets. His dad's eyes darken, and the scowl returns, deepens.

"God damn it, Jake. You don't get it!" his dad growls in his face and shakes him hard enough to make his head snap back and forth.

And, for the first time, Jake begins to wonder about ZimZim. His dad's message begins to sink in.

After that, he stops talking about ZimZim and when his dad asks he says there is no such thing as imaginary friends. Slowly, he realizes ZimZim is just another part of him. ZimZim is him.

* * *

"I think Old Man Greene is losing it," Jesse said, turning to sit so that one leg falls over each side of the wall, not even bothering to count the gnomes anymore.

"What do you mean?"

"He's just—weird. Ever since Peter Randolph and Kyle Murdoch messed up his lawn, he's been really paranoid about kids walking by. More paranoid than usual, I mean."

Jake dropped his eyes to the ground, losing track of his gnome count. "That is weird."

"He threatened me with a shovel the other day. I thought he was gonna take a swing at me or something. He's a fucking nutter."

"A fucking *what?*"

"Nutter. I heard it in a movie my parents were watching the other night. You know…" Jesse stood up stiffly and raised his nose in the air, putting on his best British accent impersonation: "That there, my good man, is a fucking nutter."

Jake doubled over laughing, nearly falling off the wall. "A fucking nutter," he imitated.

And then they're both laughing, Jake and his friend Jesse — the gnomes, and the curiosity at their number, forgotten.

*   *   *

He is a baby, looking up. The faces of his mom and dad loom over him like floating balloons. They say things and he feels loved and comforted and safe.

His parents — mom and dad — tuck him into the blanket to keep him warm and then they're gone. The light is dimmed so that only a soft blue glow wafts up to him from across the room.

He sleeps.

He awakens once during the night and a face he doesn't recognize is up there in the space over him. The face looks down at him and smiles. The face says something, and then chuckles lightly.

He stares up at this strange face, and, as he watches, the face begins to change. It twists and folds and the eyes grow large and black and runny.

He jerks awake suddenly and looks up. The strange

face is gone.
That — is his earliest memory.

* * *

Jesse grinned at Jake. "Let's just say there are thirty-four. Who gives a fuck anyway?"

"Okay. They're just a bunch of stupid gnomes."

"Yeah. Let's go home."

Jake grinned back at Jesse. His accent was terrible, but he tried it anyway: "Those gnomes are all a bunch of fucking nutters if you ask me, don't you say, old chap?"

Together, they burst into laughter.

* * *

The next day at school, Jesse's seat was empty.

TWENTY

"Don't you have to go home sometime?"

"Do I? This isn't home? Er, I mean, this is basically like my home, being here with you."

They were sitting on the couch watching TV. Harlan looked over at Grace; he was so happy to have her back — his heart warmed just thinking about her — he was glad she was alive, glad to have a kindred spirit by his side, but there was something wrong, something was bothering him.

"I'm just glad you're okay," Harlan said. "You can stay as long as you want. You know I like having you around. Fuck work; the company is doing just fine without me."

On the TV a commercial came on for the *Seventeenth Wild West Rodeo and Festival*. Images of men in cowboy hats on horses cavorted across the screen; lassos being thrown; children clapping at a rodeo clown; torches being lit; sausages served skewered on sticks; carnival games; fireworks. He'd taken Jake to that festival once, just him and his son. If he remembered correctly, they'd both become sick from eating some bad hotdogs and had to go home early.

The "wild west" stuff always reminded him of *his* father, the one he hadn't spoken with in years and Jake had never met. He could still picture his father, what he looked like with his hat and boots atop one of the horses, scowling down at him.

"Where shall we go to dinner tonight?" Grace asked.

"I don't know. Any ideas?"

"What about that one place, uh, with the lasagna? What was it called? And they had the most amazing garlic bread…"

"What? Luigi's? The Italian place? We went there last night."

"Oh, we did?"

Harlan shook his head. "How about a sandwich?"

"Okay."

Harlan got up and went to the kitchen. He opened the fridge and began to collect things on the counter for the sandwiches—the bread, some turkey slices, a packet of Swiss cheese, a greasy bottle of mayonnaise—and began to assemble them. He poured himself another couple of fingers of scotch and wondered if Grace was going to be weird all week. He was supposed to have Jake this weekend and he didn't want his son to feel uncomfortable. Maybe she had a concussion.

"Hey, Grace?"

"Yes?"

"What would you think if I took you in to see a doctor; you know, just to have you checked out?"

"A doctor? I'd rather not."

"It's okay. I'll call my guy, Dr. Weaveler, and get you in as soon as possible. He's a friend of mine. He'll take good care of you."

Harlan returned to the living room with the sandwiches on a couple of plates. He handed one to Grace, who took it tentatively.

"Need another drink?" Harlan asked.

"No. I'm fine. Thank you."

As soon as he was finished with his sandwich, he'd call up Dr. Weaveler.

They ate in silence, watching the TV.

*   *   *

"Yes, Harlan. Oh God. Right there!"

He was on top again and she was moaning beneath him. He thrust and she was very wet, so wet he could hardly feel himself. It was like sliding in and out of some sort of exquisite oil.

"Oh, fuck me, Harlan. Yes!"

He couldn't remember how he'd gotten here. He'd blacked out again. But, for the moment, it didn't seem to matter. He was with Grace and that was what counted.

She pushed her hips up to meet him, and then bucked him up and over and she was on top, her thighs grinding over him. He looked into her eyes, but Grace was somewhere else, looking up, biting her lip. He reached up and grasped her breasts with his hands; they were cold as he mashed them in his warm and sweaty palms.

For a moment, it was like he was somewhere else. The bedroom began to fade, becoming translucent, and the bed felt different on his back and buttocks. The air was warm and stifling. Heat lines rippled and distorted the room so that it appeared to him like an underground dream, the walls like the rock and packed earth of a subterranean grotto. He could smell pungent earth and rot and there was a chamber he was looking down on from above filled with detritus, like a junk yard.

A coldness spread through him. He pushed Grace off of him. He wrapped his fingers into her hair and yanked her down to the bed. She moaned. He backhanded her across the face and she writhed with pleasure. He flipped her over and began to fuck her from behind, hard; bruising hard.

"Yes, Harlan. Do what you want with me. I'm yours. Yes...Yes!"

He raked her back with his nails.

He could feel himself getting close.

*   *   *

She was so wet, so soft.

When he'd been young—still in high school, he thought, or maybe early college—he'd had a brief two week relationship with a girl who'd had a short androgynous haircut and slim, milky legs. She had been much shorter than he and, because of that, the sex had been interesting. He had been able to lift her and flip her in ways he'd not been able to do with any woman he'd been with since, and he'd taken advantage of it; he'd been inexperienced so, naturally, he'd experimented. After their first night together, during their morning quickie, she had begun her period. Of course, he had been young then and she had been young — their hormones like a rumbling fire — so they had continued to have sex, even through the following week, as messy as it had been.

He remembered that slick, warm feeling, the extra lubrication the blood provided. And the smell; the animal sweats and fluids of the body mingling with the phosphorous metallic odor that hung in the air like a rusty spray. You could almost see it, the air filtered through floating red particles, and, he remembered, that smell, to him — his parents having brought him up to be a God-fearing Christian — had brought to mind the smoldering of brimstone, and he relished it.

He thrust into her. His eyes were closed. He was close, rumbling, building.

He came, pushing hard one final time, pushing deep as he climaxed.

He sighed heavily, panting. He opened his eyes.

At first, he was not sure what he was looking at. Things were red and squiggly. He pulled out and the sensation was like pulling himself from a pot of honey or gelatin, sucking at him. Something wet and heavy fell to the bed. He was sticky. His still-erect penis was smeared in sticky gray matter and blood. Grace remained bent before him, on her hands and knees; she was open, a flap of flesh hanging between her legs, torn down her belly so that he could see pulsing inside her.

He jerked back, thinking: *What the fuck is that?*

The smell hit him and he gagged. He flopped over the side of the bed, and vomited.

"Oh, fuck! *Fuck!*"

He stood and backed away from the bed, saliva threads dripped from his chin.

"Damn, that was good."

Grace turned over to lie on her side.

He took another step back. Grace's eyes slid up to meet his.

"I know we don't really have one of *those* kind of relationships, but..." she bit her lip, pausing.

Harlan took another step back. Grace was pale, so pale; she had a couple of dark spots beginning to bloom on her face and her neck was a swollen purple choker. The spot on her lip, where she'd bit it, was indented and white.

Grace's eyes rolled upwards, then, reluctantly, come back around. "Er. What was I saying?"

Harlan couldn't speak. *What the fuck? What the fuck? Fuck!*

"Oh. Right. I just wanted to say something. We're really good together, don't you think?"

He couldn't move; he was frozen in place.

Grace bit her lip again, coyly, and her teeth actually sank into her flesh a little. "Harlan," she said.

He could feel the cold creeping up his leg again, threatening another blackout, and this time, he welcomed it.

"I love you."

TWENTY-ONE

This last week at his mom's house had been the strangest one yet. He'd seen some things—things he was almost sure couldn't be real. It was a relief, then, to be getting away for a while, getting away from the creek and his walks to and from school and his strange dreams, even if only for the weekend, escaping to his dad's place.

His mom was distant, as usual, but, surprisingly, she hadn't been drinking. She was just very distracted, preoccupied with something, and it showed.

He sat in the passenger's seat, looking out the window listlessly.

"Are you looking forward to spending time with your dad this week, Jake?" his mom asked, but her heart wasn't in it.

"Actually, yeah. I hope he's in a good mood."

"I'm sure he will be."

"Yeah."

Outside the window, he watched a couple of boys on their bikes attempting to pedal up the hill just outside his neighborhood. It looked like they were headed for the gas station corner store at the top of the hill. As the incline became steeper, he could see them begin to struggle and huff, slowing, until eventually the smaller of the two boys was forced to jump off his bike and walk it the rest of the way. When the larger boy reached the top of the rise, he jumped off his bike and stood there waiting for the smaller boy. Jake couldn't hear them, but it looked as if the larger boy was jeering at the smaller boy, making fun of him for getting off his bike too early. Jake supposed they were brothers. He wondered what it would be like to have a little brother, what he could show him.

"Do you have any homework you need to get done this weekend, Jake?"

"A little."

"Okay. Just make sure not to forget about it. I know it's easy to get distracted at your father's place."

"Sure, Mom."

*　　*　　*

At first, his dad had seemed normal.

"Hey, buddy. How was your week?"

"It was good, I guess."

Jake tossed his backpack behind the couch and flopped himself down.

"You want a snack or something?" his dad said.

"No. I'm okay."

His dad wandered to the kitchen anyway. He expected to hear this dad pouring a drink, but there was only silence.

"Hey, Dad?"

"Yes?" His dad's voice was deep and phlegmy, like he needed to clear his throat.

"It smells funny in here."

His dad sounded distracted. "Does it?"

Silence in the apartment.

"Hey, Dad?"

"Yes?"

"I'm going to go play in the back, in my room, if that's okay?"

"Fine. That's fine. Just don't go in my room. It's… I'm working on something…"

It was like being in the same house with a stranger.

Jake wandered down the hallway. The room his dad had deemed "Jake's room" was at the end of the hall. He passed by his dad's room; the door was closed. He thought he heard something; stopped; listened; then hurried along to his room. He shut the door firmly behind him.

He had heard something: a sort of wet scraping.

His room was small, but cozy, and Jake had always felt comfortable here. He turned the TV on and settled himself on the bed to watch some Saturday afternoon television. After a while, he dozed.

Later, he dug out his sketchpad and began to mess around. For the first time in days he felt like working on his board game. "The Cave of Mystery" he called it, a game of "high action adventure." He smiled as he wrote this out on a clean sheet in his sketchpad, making a logo for his game. He began to draw around it, etching an image of the cave's skull mouth opening and the Fuggle Brothers, grinning and frowning respectively, dancing on the page.

His dad never came to see if he wanted something for dinner and, after a while, his stomach began to rumble. He ventured out of the room. It was dark, the day had faded to night some hours ago, and none of the lights were on in the house. He flipped the hallway light on and tiptoed in his socks; he passed his dad's bedroom, the door still closed, no light leaking beneath it. He made his way through the living room and to the kitchen. The place was too quiet and felt deserted. His dad must have gone to bed.

He made himself a sandwich and, putting it on a plate, snagged a Coke from the fridge and tiptoed back to his room.

In the comfort of the cozy room, he devoured his sandwich and drank his Coke. For a while, he stayed up playing video games. Then he went to bed.

He dreamed.

*   *   *

He walks slowly on the padded sand. He can feel the soft grit on the soles of his bare feet. The creek bed is vast, otherworldly, stretching out from him; the tanned and textured sand; the rivulets like stratifying veins; the sky above a looming marble dome; the trees to either side grown vaster, ancient, obscuring his view of the houses and apartments from his neighborhood that must surely still be there. The only sound in the air is the breeze, wail-

ing faintly around him, and the damp flop of his feet, kicking the sticky sand about.

He is alone and aimless; he can feel it. The world is a pressure that surrounds him. He looks about and he breathes deeply of the amber air. He feels comfortable and relaxed; nothing is out of place. He is confident in his singularity, and content.

After a while, the ground becomes softer, wetter; he can feel the slop sucking at the bottoms of his feet. He enters a swampy area and begins to zig and zag in order to avoid the sunken holes of fetid water. There are things in the water, but that doesn't matter; right now, it means nothing to him. Phosphorous patches bloom in spots of clustered flies, buzzing happily in the murk.

Passing the swamp, he stumbles upon a path of sorts, an indented trough of dirt carved into the upward sloping hillocks of shivering yellow grass. He follows the path, the dirt beginning to warm his feet, as he crests the top of the hill and catches sight of his destination: Sherwood Forest. The path twists and wriggles and disappears into the copse of trees, between two of the largest trunks, plunging into shadow like the open maw of a cave. Only then – upon sight of the forest – does he begin to feel something stirring within him, a trepidation, a foreboding sense of dislocation.

Stepping over the threshold into the shade of the trees, the temperature is noticeably cooler. There is a dank smell in the air, loamy and organic; the smell of turned earth. He steps amongst the trees, standing in the grove where he has spent many hours playing. A piece of wood is nailed into a nearby tree; his eyes follow the sporadic wooden cuts up into the branches, where a single slat of wood remains hanging by a couple of rusty nails. He stares at the last remains of the tree house him and Jesse built a year or two ago, now only a couple of forlorn wooden planks, worn away to nothing. It's as if time has passed, yet he stands here the same nine-year-old boy he's always been.

He continues to walk, wherever his feet dare to take him. Into the forest, into a dense patch of foliage that crowds the narrow path before him, one he has not noticed before. It is even darker here, and he soon finds himself stepping into another open area, a small dark patch of earth shunned of plant growth. At its center lies a massive tree trunk, snaking roots like clawing appendages hungrily seeking to hide their heads in the obscurity and sustenance of the soil. The tree, however, doesn't appear to be alive, its dark leafless branches flailing into the browning overgrowth, belonging to an ancient species extinct from this world, its skeletal remnants evidence of different times long past. At its center, there is an opening, a cavernous entrance into blackness.

He crouches; taking to his hands and knees, and crawls through the opening and into the dark and damp tunnel.

Inside, the smell of turned earth is almost overwhelming, a deep, moist ashy pungency. The unseen soil beneath his knees and hands is soft, squishy in places. As the entrance behind him fades into the dark, his eyes become adjusted to a faint warming luminescence. There isn't space in the tunnel for him to turn around now. He keeps moving.

He comes to another opening, no bigger than the tunnel, and plunges through it. He slides down a small muddy incline into a much larger tunnel. A cluster of unreal-looking mushrooms hug the earthen wall by him. He is able to stand now, wondering vaguely if the mushrooms are the kind you can eat. The tunnel branches in two directions *and he picks one at random, his feet in the squelching mud.*

The tunnel twists to the right, then slightly to the left. It is impossible to tell how long he walks before he comes to the tunnel's end, a curving wall of smeared mud, a misshapen door set into the earth at a canted angle. The door is large and elaborate and clearly very old. He reaches out and tries the doorknob, but it won't turn, won't budge the slightest bit. He peers upward along the face of the dark, inlaid wood, to an intricate brass door knocker, a heavy swiveled striker that hangs beneath two round bolts indented in the molded metal that gives the knocker the appearance of having a sort of sagging face. He grasps the warm metal and knocks – once, twice; a third time.

Nothing happens. He presses his ear against the door and is surprised by how warm the wood is, much warmer than the side of the tunnel he resides in; the heat must be coming from the other side. And then, as he listens, he thinks he can hear something, a scraping, something applying pressure from the other side.

He pulls his head back and steps away from the door. A deep dread rises up in him, though he doesn't know why. He has a sense of standing on the threshold, of being close to something inexplicable. Some doors are not meant to be opened, he thinks. He turns, and goes back the way he came.

He takes the other tunnel, and soon finds himself on a steadily descending decline, spiraling to the right. The air becomes heavier, muggy with moisture, and he begins to sweat. He pushes onward, until the tunnel levels out and another opening materializes through the murky air, illuminated from within. He steps up to this opening, and peers inside.

The light is coming from above, orange and warm, like

that from a heat lamp; he can feel it between the hairs on the top of his head, tingling in his scalp. A vast structure rises before him – twisting precariously up into the hazy light, disappearing beyond the reach of his eyes – made from all manner of various things, lashed together by haphazard lines of rope, and cloth, and, in some places, partially rusted wire. The first thing he recognizes, perhaps ten feet up the pile, is the shape of an old wooden dresser with brass knobs in a similar style to those belonging to the door from earlier; he can also make out the sides and ends of other pieces of furniture: an end table flipped upside down, a crumpled and disfigured wad of bed springs, a large wardrobe, a wooden bed leg carved with birds spiraling around and around. And there are other things: an afghan-style blanket speared upon an elongated hat rack; couch pillows; a sprinkling of old movies caught in a plastic bag stretched to opacity; the body of an acoustic guitar; the twist of an old rug; a large lampshade suspended over an antique chair tied and hanging from the junk above it, turning faintly back and forth in the heat. And amongst the bric a brac, there are various recognizable pieces of trash: fast food bags, soda cans, boxes once containing crackers and potato chips and microwave dinners. And there are things he doesn't recognize, things obscured amongst other things. The entire mass goes up and up, a behemoth of trash, each piece carefully stacked and arranged and tied into place.

He steps closer, entering the room completely. Besides the towering castle of junk that disappears upwards without a ceiling in sight, the room is only moderately sized, the walls curving roughly around, made from the same plastered earth of the tunnels he's left behind. Perhaps, he thinks, there is another tunnel on the other side. He begins to move off to the right, but before he takes more than a couple of steps, there is a rustling and a scratching sound coming from high above. He stops, listens, and waits, the sound coming down, nearer and nearer.

The sound is somewhere amongst the lower furniture now; for a moment he hears the scrape of some bells or a muted wind chime pushed against a gritty surface. Then, he is able to place the sound. Whatever it is has reached the other side of the old wooden dresser; there is a click, and the sound of something being slid out of the way, then, a small door belonging to a nearby wardrobe falls open perhaps ten feet above him. For a moment, there is only darkness. Then, a small white head emerges, and frail, emaciated limbs pull a pale and hairless body forward. The creature peers at Jake with open curiosity, then sidles forward on all fours, pulls itself on to the chair that hangs beneath the lampshade, and sits, swinging precariously. When the chair begins to settle, the creature looks at him and smiles. Jake recognizes the creature then: it is the man from his dreams, the thing he calls the Melting Man.

For a moment, they only look at each other, each assessing the other. Then, the Melting Man speaks: "You came on your own. I've underestimated you."

Jake licks his lips. "Where am I?"

"Neither here nor there, but somewhere in between," the Melting Man says, that smile never leaving his face.

"That's not really an answer."

"You didn't ask a real question."

Jake eyes the Melting Man suspiciously. "Why don't you come down from there?"

That smile flickers, only for a moment. "I could never do that."

"Why not?"

"I'm forbidden. I cannot set foot on such ground. Not

ever again."

"But I've seen you, above ground in the forest."

"Yes. I can send you visions, glimpses of my world, but never enter yours. Not in my own flesh anyway. Unless… but it is too soon for such things. Why have you come?"

Jake gasps. "Why? I…just wandered in here."

A tiny crease mars the smoothness of the Melting Man's forehead for a moment. "That's not possible. You were looking for me, right?"

"Uh…I guess so…"

The Melting Man's face smooths itself again and he leans forward, sticking his head even farther out upon his neck. "And now that you've found me, what is your plan?"

Jake thinks for a moment. He is sure he must be dreaming; he can't take any of this too seriously. "I only want to know who you are. What do you want from me?"

"But that's two separate questions." The mockery in his voice is thinly veiled; Jake can sense a suppressed contempt in the Melting Man's every word.

"Alright – who are you?"

"My name is, sadly, forgotten. I'm from a place called the Cu'rboros Urad, on the edge of the Veiled Sea. But that was a long time ago. Now, I am a prisoner. And I need your help."

"I've never heard of such a place."

"I'm not surprised." The Melting Man leans even farther forward, the chair tilting and straining so that it looks like he might fall, or the chair snap from its bonds. "Will you help me?"

"I…What can I do?"

The Melting Man leans back, the ropes holding the chair creaking as he settles. He brings his pale hand up and turns it, looking at it; he picks something from a nail.

After a moment, he speaks. "I need you to play a part for me, a very important role."

"A part? What do you mean?"

"In the Masque." The Melting Man's grin seems to split his face.

Jake has no idea what the Melting Man is talking about. "The mask?"

"Yes – The Masquerade. Will you help me?"

"I don't understand." The Melting Man only looks down at him, face washed of expression, waiting.

Reluctantly, "I guess," Jake says. "If I can, I mean."

"Good!" The Melting Man jumps, claps his hands and holds them together, as if giving himself a handshake. The chair swings violently forward and back. "Good. Yes. Excellent."

Jake watches the Melting Man nearly slide from his perch, but the pale creature grasps the back of the chair at the last second and holds on, his smile turning to a sudden grimace of effort as he pulls himself back, sitting again, waiting for the chair to settle its precarious swinging.

When the chair finally settles to a slow rocking, like the pendulum in a grandfather clock, the Melting Man says to him, "I knew you would help me, if only you saw the horrible state I'm in here."

"I still don't understand. What can I do?"

The Melting Man leans forward again, his head protruding out on his neck. "I will ask a favor of you, sometime soon, and you must help me."

"What is it?"

Eyes slant, "It won't be anything difficult. There's no need for you to worry. I only need your help to escape from here, from this filthy cell. You can see that can't you? How disgusting this place is?"

Jake nods.

"Good."

The rest of the dream — the return journey, if there was one — he is unable to remember when he wakes up.

*　　*　　*

Jake remembered a scene in one of the movies his dad owned where, in a dream, a man had walked through a graveyard and had had a conversation with a dead person. In the morning, the man had awoken in bed, pulled the covers aside, and found the sheets muddied, his feet caked with cemetery dirt. Jake half-expected this to be true of his own dream, but, when he pulled the sheets aside — the light from the Sunday morning sun slanting into the little bedroom at his dad's apartment — his feet had been clean, the light making them shine bare and white. It was just another one of his dreams. It already felt like a distant memory, the details fading into the hazy morning.

His dad came out of his bedroom only once that day, only to answer the door when his mom came to pick him up.

"Dad? Are you okay?"

"Yes, son. I'm fine."

"Are you sure?"

For a moment, his dad looked down at him and their eyes met; his dad's eyes clouded. Then, it was gone, and Jake wondered if he'd seen anything at all.

"Yes, son. I'm fine."

In the car with his mom, he thought about it, and realized he'd seen something more. For a second, his dad had looked as if he was going to wink at him.

Walking away, he turned to see his dad standing in the doorway, wearing the faintest of smiles, a knowing smile — they shared a secret.

PART THREE: FIRE

TWENTY-TWO

Slowly, Harlan awoke, drooling on himself.

He looked around. He was in his apartment, the blinds shuttered closed on every window. The place was dark and damp and rancid, like a cavern. He stood. The television was left on, mindlessly broadcasting static into the room. He'd been what? Watching TV?

He wobbled into the kitchen. He felt weak—an empty shell of himself—the dragging exhaustion of a long and hard binge. He opened the fridge and grabbed the first thing he saw, a greasy packet of lunch meat. He began to gobble the meat with both hands.

He finished what was left of the meat, snatched a Coke from the fridge, drank down most of it in a few gulps, and left the can with the used up and empty lunch meat bag on the counter. He belched loudly.

It wasn't until he began to shuffle back to the living room he began to wonder about things. Had Jake been here? What day was it? What had he been doing? He began to remember things: little flashes.

Come here, bitch! he'd said.

What do you say to this, bitch! he'd said.

He'd jumped around, flailing his arms like a school boy. He'd been hooting and hollering and mumbling things. He'd danced about. He'd celebrated.

What the fuck was going on?

He couldn't remember any of this, not clearly.

A loud scraping sound startled him from his thoughts. He jumped, his eyes shooting up to the source of the noise.

The television had shifted forward in its wooden display.

He froze, waiting for it to happen again. Nothing.

Hadn't he just turned the TV off just a second ago? The static glow cast a pall over the room.

He walked over to the couch and sat down. He was shaking all over, trying to remember what had been happening to him. He held his knees with his hands to keep them from shaking too violently.

That grating, scraping sound jarred him again.

He looked up just in time to see the TV set settle forward.

He could see himself, in his mind's eye, thrusting and thrusting. He'd come and then settled back, already stroking himself, building up to go again. He'd been sticky and stained. The figure on the bed next to him had been motionless.

This time he actually saw the TV jitter forward so that it was leaning, almost toppling over the edge of the television stand. The screen flickered; an image came into focus. It was the room with the red curtain and the stone altar. The two men entered the screen, one from each side. One of them grinned, while the other frowned. They turned their faces in his direction and looked at him—actually looked at him, not at the camera, their eyes meeting his—and they brought their hands up, and, simultaneously, waved at him.

Harlan groaned.

Then, the picture began to blur; the TV began to warp, bubbling outward, melting down the front of the cabinet. A face appeared for a moment, and then flashed away. The face flickered back into existence. Grace looked out the screen, out at him. "Harlan," she said. "Listen. I don't have much time."

Harlan stared; his eyes felt as if they might bulge and pop from their sockets. "Oh shit," he said.

"You have to fight it. He can get to you now. Harlan! Listen to me! You have to fight!"

"Grace?"

He remembered suddenly: a flash of the scene in his bedroom. Grace was on her back on the bed, torn open; blood on the sheets, walls, everywhere; a gelatinous liquid pooling beneath her, running off the bed onto the floor. There was a bloody hole in her stomach where he'd been mindlessly fucking her.

The TV flashed, blinding him utterly, and he heard it crash to the floor.

"Grace?"

He could feel the cold spreading up his body, threatening to take control. He pushed it back, and, for the moment, it subsided. Grace was right: he had to fight whatever the fuck this was.

As his vision slowly came back to him, he listened. His apartment was very still without the broadcast glow of the television screen. Silent. Dark.

TWENTY-THREE

Jess didn't want to raise the baby alone. She touched her stomach, expecting a bulge, like it was when she was pregnant with Jake, but there was nothing—of course there was nothing. She could have an abortion, she thought—this child of her twisted ex-boyfriend—but she wouldn't. She had the money and the resources to raise another child and she didn't think she was too old; she would be fine. And Harlan would help; he was a very good father to Jake, a better parent than she.

Harlan.

She turned out of the parking lot of the grocery store, and merged into traffic.

More and more she wished she could have worked things out with Harlan. Why hadn't it worked? What had they fought over? Stupid things. She couldn't even remember what they were; couldn't have told anyone now, if she'd been stopped and asked, why her marriage hadn't worked out, why she'd felt so vehemently sure of herself when she'd signed the divorce papers. She wondered if she'd made a mistake. She wondered what Harlan, who'd resisted her threats of divorce over and over again, thought about their split now; what could he think of her.

By the time she got home, pulling the car up the driveway and into the garage, she was crying. She couldn't help herself. It wasn't like her to lose control like this, but she felt so helpless, so lost; so alone. She let the tears fall.

She killed the ignition, got out of the car, walked around to the other side to get her groceries. She took her groceries through the door and into the kitchen, set the plastic sacks on the counter, then went back to push the button to close the garage door. She returned to the kitchen and began to unpack her purchases.

By the time she was done unpacking the groceries, she was in control of herself again. She wiped the tears from her puffy eyes.

Damn, she needed a drink.

A few years ago, Jake, only a toddler of three or four at the time, had stumbled into the house wailing over a scraped knee. She'd been in the kitchen fixing lunch and she'd rushed out, hugged him and told him it would be okay, not to worry, it was just a scrape, it wasn't deep. But Jake's screaming had continued, more from the horror of the welling blood and black grit in the wound than from the pain. She'd told him not to move, that she'd be right back with a bandage and something to wash the wound with, and run down the hall to the bathroom. She'd gathered the supplies as quickly as she could — some gauze, a washcloth, some disinfectant — and raced back to where she'd left her screaming son in the entryway over the tiled floor where he wouldn't drip blood on the carpet. When she'd returned — she'd only been gone a minute — Harlan had been kneeling down by their son and Jake had stopped crying, he was even smiling a little. Harlan had placed a tissue over Jake's knee. Then Harlan began to hobble around, pretending his own knee was wounded. "Oh, no! He's crippled for life! He'll never walk again!" Jake's smile had widened; a small giggle had even escaped him. Harlan had that effect on Jake; he could stop their son's misery with a glance, or a face. Jess had brought her medical supplies over, but she was too late; Harlan had already saved the day, and made Jake happy again.

Jess smiled to herself, placing the milk in the door of the fridge. She'd always been a little jealous of the bond Harlan and Jake had, that she didn't seem able to share. But her jealousy seemed silly to her now, when she thought about it. Harlan was a good father and Jake was lucky to have him. "I want to be a better father than my dad was," Harlan used to say. "I don't know — I just don't want to turn into a judgmental asshole. I want to have a real relationship with my son." Harlan rarely talked about his past and when he said things like this Jess always remembered them.

She thought of a time when Jake had been only weeks old, a tiny baby in the crib across the room, and she and Harlan had fallen asleep on the couch, her leaned against his chest, him with his arm wrapped around her. When Jake had begun to cry, Harlan had gently laid her aside and gone to their newborn son, letting her sleep, but she'd still been awake, exhausted with her eyes closed. When Harlan had quieted Jake, settling their baby back to sleep, Jess had heard Harlan whispering to himself as he crossed the room back to her. He'd sighed. "God you're beautiful," he'd said, thinking she was asleep and couldn't hear him. "This is perfect. This is the life I always wanted."

Jess closed the refrigerator door. The only alcohol she had in the house was a bottle of wine tucked away in one of the cabinets. She could picture its smooth, elongated form where it sat—dark, dusty, pushed back amongst other forgotten things like the food processor and the fancy plates and silverware she and Harlan had received as wedding gifts and that she used to bring out on Thanksgiving and Christmas.

She shook herself. What time was it? She glanced at the time on the microwave. Jake wouldn't be home from school for another couple of hours.

Her eyes strayed to the telephone on the wall. She could call him. What would be the harm?

She picked up the receiver, hesitated, and then dialed the number.

The phone rang once; twice. On the third ring she changed her mind, and was about to hang up, when a voice picked up.

"Yes?"

At first, she didn't recognize his voice. "Harlan?" she tried tentatively.

"Uh...yes?"

"It's Jessica. How are you?"

The voice softened. "Jessica! I'm well. How are you?"

"I'm good." She stopped, wasn't sure what to say next, how to ask.

But Harlan surprised her. "Jessica?" he said. "Would it be okay if I came over, just for a little while?"

He'd asked for her. "Okay," she said.

"I'll be right over."

The dial tone filled her ear. She replaced the receiver in its wall dock.

She sighed. Harlan wanted to come over — that was a good sign. It was about time they had a heart to heart talk.

TWENTY-FOUR

Jake walked briskly, happy to be done with another droning day. School sucked without Jesse to
pass him notes when the teacher's back was turned,
to hang out with at lunchtime, to joke around with
and lighten the mood. It had been three days. Jesse
must be home sick, Jake thought; probably had the
flu or something.

Last night, Jake had thought he'd seen one of those
stupid gnomes from Mrs. Marlow's yard under the
dining room table. The little guy was crouched down
in the shadows and his mother was sitting at the
table reading something—her legs fidgety, crossing
and uncrossing—the gnome right there in the corner,
drooling a little, watching his mom's feet. Jake had
dropped to the floor to get a better look, crawling forward, and the gnome had turned its ugly face up to
look at him. The little guy's facial expression hadn't

changed. Jake had crawled under the table from the other side and the gnome had fallen back, disappearing into the shadows. When he'd reached the corner he'd found it empty. He'd looked around more closely and found something tucked against the table leg, something small and cold: a Zippo-style lighter, the nicest one he'd ever seen. He'd held it in his hand, feeling its weight; the smooth brushed aluminum; the plain, dark coolness of it.

He'd flicked it open and the click it had made was surprisingly loud. His mom had shrieked and jumped, barking her knee on the bottom of the table.

"My God, Jake!" his mom had said, grimacing, staring down at him, eyes wide. "What are you doing down there?"

"Nothing."

"What is that?"

"Uh, it's nothing."

"Give it here."

Jake had handed his mom the lighter from under the table.

"You found this down there?"

"Yeah."

His mom had paused, looking the lighter over. "I'm sorry, Jake, but I'm going to have to take this. It's way too dangerous. We don't need you lighting any more fires around here."

*   *   *

"Jake!"

Startled from his thoughts, he turned to see who had called his name. Jesse was behind him, running

173

up the sidewalk.

Jesse caught up to him, held out his fist and Jake met it with his own. "Jesse! What's going on? Where've you been? I haven't seen you at school."

"I've been around. What have you been doing?"

Jake shrugged. "Just got out of school. Walking home."

"Did I miss anything of importance?" Jesse asked strangely, as if he'd been gone for more than just a couple days, his face plastered with a huge grin.

"Not really."

Jesse clapped his hands together. "I didn't think so." He grinned some more.

"I looked for you online, thought we could play some Call of Duty, thought you might be bored sitting around the house being sick all day."

"Sorry about that. I've been busy."

"Doing what?"

"Would you like to see?"

"Sure."

Jesse waved his arm for Jake to follow. "Come on." He started to jog. "Let me show you something." Then, he took off up the sidewalk, breaking into a run.

Jake chased after him, his backpack bouncing on his shoulders.

They tore up the street, detouring through a patch of weeds to skirt around some of the other kids from school. Jesse ran fast and Jake had to push himself not to fall behind. They ran past Mrs. Marlow's yard without a second glance.

Then, a little ahead of him, Jesse stopped in front of Old Man Greene's house, and turned to wait for

Jake to catch up.

Jesse was still grinning from ear to ear when Jake caught up to him. "What are we doing here?"

Jesse can barely contain himself. "You're going to like this. You're going to really like this. Come on." He stepped onto Old Man Greene's lawn.

"Jesse—what are you doing?" His voice was sharper than he meant it to be.

Jesse walked up the lawn, ignoring his plea, still waving for him to follow.

Jake took a step, one foot sinking into the soft grass, the other still tethered to the sidewalk. He heard the crash of Greene's door being flung open and quickly pulled his foot back. From his spot on the sidewalk, he watched Jesse strolling casually across the yard. Old Man Greene stepped out onto his porch, shovel in hand.

"Shit," Jake mumbled.

Old Man Greene looked tired and angry, his hair a disheveled mess, his eyes bloodshot and staring, knuckles gone white where he gripped the shovel. He looked crazy, the kind of crazy that drove men to beat their wives, the kind of crazy that led to extreme violence, to kids being killed and buried in the yard—things like that, Jake thinks.

Jake watched in horror as Jesse walked right up to the old man. Greene raised his shovel for a moment; his eyes rolled, then came back. Jesse didn't say anything, just grinned, seemingly oblivious to Greene's anger, the color rising in the old man's cheeks. For a moment, Jake thought he was going to see it happen: that, standing here on the sidewalk, he would witness the shovel being lifted, and swung; the sharp metal in a wide arc, the sun glinting against it for a split-second, then coming forward; a dull clunk; a flash of red as something split; Jesse crumbling to the ground; a loud guffaw of triumph.

The shovel sagged in Old Man Greene's hands. Greene looked about wildly, ignoring Jesse, as if searching for something in the dark, something he couldn't see. His eyes panned over the area, hovered over Jake for a second, and then continued their scan without a second glance.

"Jake," Jesse called. "It's okay. Come on up."

Jake hesitated, thought of running, turning tail and getting the hell out of there, but his curiosity was too strong. He longed to understand what was going on. He took a step onto the grass, then another. He began to walk up the lawn towards Jesse, Old Man Greene still on the porch only a few feet from his friend. For a second, Greene tensed, and then seemed to relax a little, making no sign of stopping Jake from continuing.

He came forward. Jesse didn't move, flashing that ridiculous grin in his direction; Greene stood in place, his shoulders heaving up and down as if he were breathing hard. The lawn was not in the condition it used to be: it was lumpy, too soft under his feet. There were patches of upturned earth, yellowing grass, as if much of the sod had been torn up and replaced in a haphazard and hurried fashion. From the street it looked as if Greene had stopped caring for it and let it go to seed—from within the yard it was much worse, torn and shredded, as if a horde of football players had run laps upon it in their cleat-spiked feet.

He stopped, still several yards away from the front porch where Old Man Greene stood.

Jesse said, "Hey, Jake, I want to show you what I've been working on."

The door stood open behind Greene, dark and shadowy inside.

He looked at the old man; Greene looked back, his face pinched, the shovel remained placid in his hands.

"What?" Jake said, feeling slow, stupid.

Old Man Greene stepped aside, opening a pathway up the steps and into the dark staleness of his house.

Jesse was right beside him. "Come on, Jake. Come and see."

Jake began to go up the steps, Jesse beside him, coaxing him. "There we go. Come on in."

Jake stepped onto the porch; the old wood creaked beneath his feet, rusty nail on wood. He glanced over at Old Man Greene. The old man stood there, looking helpless. His eyes were watery, submissive, and pleading.

"Come on, Jake. That's it."

Jake stood before the open doorway. He tried to see inside, but he could see little more than the coatless coat rack on the wall just inside the house and the tiled floor disappearing into the darkness like a receding tongue at the back of one's throat and the air inside was warm and muggy, he could feel it breathing out on him — and there was something bad in the air, something fungal, like rotting fruit.

He took a step forward. His eyes began to adjust to the murk. The room was small and there was a camera perched upon a tripod like insect legs. He could just make out the lump of a table. There was an extravagant curtain pulled across the entire back wall — in the shadows its color was like a fresh bruise.

"I don't know," Jake heard the words coming out of him. "Maybe another time."

Jesse said, "It's okay, Jake. It's okay."

Jake turned. "No. I..." Jesse was standing behind him, blocking his path, still grinning, nodding his head up and down.

Jake pushed past his friend. He jumped the stairs saying, "I'll see you later, Jesse. I have to go," and he ran across the grass.

In his mind he could see Jesse pointing, sending Old Man Greene after him like a Doberman; Old Man Greene lumbering down the steps, raising the shovel up in both hands like a bat as he began to stomp across the yard, his bloodshot eyes bugging furiously, the webwork of varicose veins standing out on the backs of his large hairy fists, gaining on him, closer and closer, preparing to swing the shovel.

Jake cringed as he ran, trying to make himself small, expecting to be knocked from his feet at any moment. He nearly lost his footing in a small dirty cut in the grass, but managed to keep his feet and kept going.

When he reached the sidewalk, he risked a glance behind him. He stopped. Jesse and Old Man Greene hadn't moved; they stood where he'd left them. They had turned in his direction, watching him.

As he stared at them, Old Man Greene lifted his shovel, not in a threatening way but as he might raise his hand for a wave. "Don't let your father open the gate, Jake," he called out.

Jesse turned sharply to stare at Greene, moved to push the old man back into the house.

"He doesn't believe! Don't let them out!"

The door slammed. Jake was left alone on the street.

He turned, and ran home as fast as his legs would carry him.

TWENTY-FIVE

Jake was surprised to find both of his parents at the house when he got home. They were sitting on the couch in the living room watching TV together. They'd been drinking: the sting of it hung in the air; bottles littered the coffee table.

Jake stood in the entryway, waiting to catch his breath from running all the way home. For a moment, the room seemed to sway and buckle; a feeling of unreality fell over him, his fingers pulled nervously at the loose threads on the straps of his backpack.

"Hey, Jake," his mom said, without getting up. "Did you have a good day at school?"

His dad didn't move, continued watching the TV.

"Yeah, Mom," Jake said. "What's Dad doing here?"

"He came over to help me with some things."

"Hey, Dad," Jake said.

Without turning his head: "Hello, son."

"Would you like a snack? Something to tide you over till dinner time?" his mom asked.

"I'll find something."

"Suit yourself."

He wasn't really hungry, but he went to the kitchen anyway. He found a bag of potato chips and crept up the stairs and down the hall to his room, holding the bag as lightly as he could: the crinkling plastic seemed loud in the odd, subdued atmosphere.

Once safely ensconced in his room, with the door shut firmly behind him, he relaxed a little. He tossed his backpack to the floor. He left the bag of chips on his bed and flipped his TV on. He grabbed the game controller and lost himself in his video games for a while. He'd play until his mom called him down for dinner, he decided.

*   *   *

After a while he realized he was thirsty, so he paused his game and stood. He slunk down the stairs and made his way to the kitchen. He took a Coke from the fridge and began on his way back. Half-way across the dining room, his dad called out to him, "Hey, son."

Jake froze. His dad was getting drunk, he could tell. His dad didn't sound like himself.

"Get me another, will ya?" his dad yelled from across the room, holding his glass in the air and shaking it so that the ice cubes rattled like freshly cleaned bones.

Jake walked across the living room and took the

glass from his dad's hand. His mother held her glass out too, not saying a word, her eyes evasive and distant. Together, they looked like a painting of misery — bloodshot eyes and smeared makeup; slumped bodies; tight grimacing mouths.

"And, son…"

Jake turned.

His dad leaned forward conspiratorially, "There's a bottle of Johnny Walker in the pantry. Why don't you use that?" He waved his hand dismissively. "And don't mess around. We're thirsty." His dad sunk back into the couch.

Jake backtracked to the kitchen to fix the drinks. He dropped fresh ice cubes in the glasses and found the bottle his dad was talking about, still wrapped in a brown paper bag from the liquor store, in the pantry. He poured a little of the amber liquid into each glass and then put the bottle in the freezer.

When he turned back into the living room, a glass in each hand, his parents were standing. "Thank you, dear," his mom said, "but I think we're going to go and take a little nap now."

His dad barked laughter. "Yes," he said, "a 'nap.'" His dad pushed his mom in front, swatting her on the butt.

Jake stood aside as his parents stumbled by, and waited until he heard their bedroom door shut with a slam, before returning to the kitchen. He set the glasses of alcohol on the table and pushed them away so he wouldn't have to smell them. He got himself some water from the faucet and sat at the table. He began to doodle on one of the notepads. Even from here he could hear his parents going at it. He tried to concentrate on his drawing, but it was impossible to ignore the grunting and the wheezing, so loud, even from across the house. He'd known it would be noisy in his own room, but even out here in the kitchen? And there was something else. Was someone weeping?

After a while, his dad lurched into the kitchen, his mom trailing listlessly. His mom looked exhausted, her mascara smeared, pooling vacantly beneath her eyes. His dad's face and eyes were red, his hair oily and unkempt, his mouth a twisted grimace.

"Where'd you put that Johnny Walker?"

"In the freezer."

"What?" His dad spun, flinging the freezer door open, snatching the bottle. "That's Black Label!" His eyes blazed. "You don't put Black Label in the freezer. Christ!"

Jake stared at his dad.

"This isn't some piss-water vodka shit like your mom drinks," his dad continued. "This is Johnny Walker, God damn it!"

Jake's mom moved in to take the bottle. "Would you like ice, dear?"

Without taking his inflamed eyes from Jake, "Ice? Hell no. Why the fuck would I want ice?"

On the other side of his dad's bulk, Jake watched his mom slopping the amber liquid into a couple of fresh glasses. She held one of them out and, turning, Jake's dad snatched it from her.

"Just give me the drink, woman."

"How about spaghetti for dinner tonight?" his mom said. She was passive, acting as if Jake's dad's actions were perfectly normal and justified.

Jake stood, shocked, frozen in place.

His dad slumped against the counter next to his mom. Jake watched his dad sip his drink; eyes cast downward, anger fading from his face. Jake watched his parents, for a moment, standing in the kitchen looking gloomy and detached.

He hurried out of the kitchen. When he got to his room, he heard someone weeping again, the sound of someone talking through barely repressed sobs. He closed his bedroom door and flopped on his bed. It was like the old days, before his parent's divorce, his mom and dad drinking together, being depressed together: it was best if he stayed out of the way. He slipped a pair of headphones over his ears and cranked the volume; he closed his eyes and tried to blot out the world.

*   *   *

Towards evening, as the light outside began to wane, Jake's stomach began to rumble. He was just thinking of cracking open the bag of chips he had sitting on his dresser when his mom called him down for dinner. He groaned and went down to join his parents downstairs.

His mom had set the dining room table with three spots, each with a plate, silverware, and paper napkin. The spaghetti was served in two separate bowls at the table's center, one for pasta, the other for the marinara meat sauce; a green can of Parmesan cheese to sprinkle on top sat between them. By the time Jake had reached the table, both his mom and his dad had already finished heaping their plates and taken them into the living room to resume their spots on the couch in front of the TV.

Jake made himself a plate and was about to slink back upstairs when his dad said, "Come join us, son." Reluctantly, Jake walked into the living room, and took a position on the floor in the corner, balancing his plate in his lap.

Jake watched his parents eat. His mom ate slowly, eating very little of what was on her plate. His dad ate like a wolf, devouring the spaghetti in huge mouthfuls that hung from his mouth like ripped entrails, sauce running out the sides of his mouth and down his stubble-raked chin. He made grunting sounds as he chewed, filling the gap between bites with gulps of Johnny Walker from his smeared and greasy glass.

Jake, despite his hunger, ate only a little of what was on his plate. His parents never spoke, seemed too absorbed in the current television program, the local news. They were acting very strange.

At the first opportunity, Jake dumped his plate in the kitchen sink, and hurried back up to his room. Soon after, he heard his dad's muffled speaking; his dad sounded upset, like he was weeping.

TWENTY-SIX

Jake's plan was to stay in the protective enclosure of his room until his parents went to bed; then, maybe, in the morning, they would be okay again.

Towards the late evening, however, he had to use the bathroom, so he ventured out into the hallway. The door to the upstairs bathroom was closed; someone was using it, so he padded down the stairs as quietly as he could in his stockinged feet. It was cooler at the bottom of the stairs; most of the lights were off and the TV glared into the gloom. A vague shape lay curled on the couch: his mom. He crept to the bathroom, his bladder aching as he walked, shut the door behind him, and relieved himself.

When he was done, he flushed the toilet, ran some cold water over his hands, and stepped out of the bathroom. He stood squinting, trying to make out his mom's features in the dim lighting, but it was difficult; she was motionless; the flashes from the TV gave things an unreal quality; the room bulged and breathed.

A wet belch. He swung around to see his dad leaning against the wall at the bottom of the steps, watching him. His dad's eyes were dark pools in the murk and he stood like a Neanderthal — bottle of Johnny Walker in hand; only a small slosh left — his head thrust forward, lips parted the slightest bit so that the light from the TV glimmered on his teeth.

Jake could feel his heart beating; he licked his lips, his mouth suddenly dry and bitter.

"Hello, son," his dad said. His voice was sly and slurred. "It's cold in here, wouldn't you say? Why don't you go and get some firewood from the pile out back." He indicated the fireplace with his free hand. "Get this thing going."

"Dad? Are you okay?"

"Go get the wood, son."

"It's not that cold. We could just…"

"Are you going to get the wood or do I have to make you?" His dad's eyes were like glass, staring down at him darkly.

Jake moved. He went out the back door and around the house to the wood pile. He peeled the blue tarp that protected the wood from the weather back from one side so that he could grab a few of the split logs. With his arms full, he made his way back to the door. It was really a nice night, the air crisp and fragrant; the stars particularly bright.

When he returned with the wood, his dad had already arranged crumpled balls of newspaper in the bottom of the fireplace. "Put the wood there," he said. "Here, I'll show you what to do." Jake watched his dad place the logs so that they stood against each other over the newspaper in a point. "Now," his dad said. "Your turn."

Jake stared at the lighter in his dad's outstretched hand, produced as if from nowhere. It was the one he'd found under the table, the one his mom had taken away from him, with the dark, brushed metal and the flip top and the real wick. His heart picked up its pace. Slowly, he reached out, and took the lighter from his dad's hot and sweaty palm.

Jake turned to the cold shadowy fireplace. "Light it," his dad breathed behind him. And he wanted to; where was the harm in that? Jake stepped toward the hearth. He brought the lighter up so he could look at it, flipped the top open with his free hand. He struck the wheel with his thumb, not expecting anything yet, but the orange flicker of flame sprang up immediately. He stared at the flame. He could feel his dad watching him. He brought the lighter down and set the fire to the newspaper; it burned instantly. He stepped back, admiring the hungry flames.

"Good. Now get more wood."

Jake, with an effort, tore his eyes from the fire to look at his dad's blazing face. "More?"

"All of it. Bring it all in."

"But…"

"Do what I say, son."

The lighter was growing hot in his hands, the wick still burning. He hissed, and dropped it, where it hit the floor and closed with a snap. He shook his singed fingers. He looked at his dad, and what he saw there was enough to get him moving again, leaving the lighter where it lay.

He went through the back door and around the house again. He waited by the wood pile for a moment, trying to sort things out. It had been like this before — his parents wasting their evenings drinking together, being depressed together — but something had changed. His dad, even being as drunk as he was, wasn't acting quite right.

Returning through the back door with another armload, he could hear his dad drunkenly ranting in the other room. He sounded miserable; tormented.

He took the wood into the living room and the smoke was acrid and cloying, mixed with the stench of whiskey, beginning to fog the room like a blurry memory. He ran to the fireplace, dropped the wood on the floor, and pulled the chain to open the flue. The smoke lingered, but the room became breathable.

His dad came into view, whirling to face him, his bottle now nearly empty, held casually by his side; his face glowed orange with the flickering of the flames, his forehead smudged with ash. "Go on now," his dad said. "Toss those on the fire." He brought the bottle up, threw his head back, and gulped the last of the whiskey.

Jake began to pick up the logs he'd dropped, and, one by one, threw them into the fire. Flames licked hungrily over the new wood, curling upward, bursting with fresh heat.

"More," his dad said.

"More?"

"I said all of it, son." His dad's voice was deadpan. "And I meant it."

Jake groaned, but began to turn towards the door.

A motion caught the corner of his eye. His mom was lying out on the couch, her skirt hiked up around her thighs; she held out her glass. He crossed to her and took the glass.

His mom lifted herself, and then fell back into the couch as if it required a great effort just to sit up. She opened her mouth as if to speak, and then closed it again.

"Jake," she managed.

Jake leaned down so he could hear what his mom was trying to tell him. "Go," she whispered, her voice ragged with emotion.

The glass was wrenched from his grasp and Jake felt the air move above his head, then there was a shattering crash against the wall.

"What did I say, son?" his dad bellowed over him. "Get the firewood. I'm not going to ask you again!"

Leaving his mom where she lay, he quickly crossed the living room and went for more wood.

Over the next couple of hours, Jake hauled wood into the house, building up the fire at his dad's instructions until the whole house felt like a blazing sauna. Soon, his head was pounding and his vision blurred. Every time he left and reentered the house, the television seemed louder, to blare into the room and his skull. The smoke made him cough; stung his eyes. As evening turned into night, the walls of the house seemed to glow with heat and radiance and the dancing flames tossed shadows into the corner of the living room. Soon, he was so exhausted he ceased to care why his dad was making him build a fire in the springtime. It was likely just another drunken obsession, one that would quickly be dismissed in the morning, when they could all wake up and forget this hellish evening had ever taken place. His arms were like rubber stalks; his back ached fiercely; his head continued to throb; he felt weak and near to passing out as he brought in the last of the wood. After that, he made his way up the stairs and down the hall like a phantom, his dad dismissing him with a wave, barely conscious of the stifling heat. At one point he heard the crying again, or was it laughter?

He flopped into his bed. His head spun and the room pulsed. Something felt out of place, something very wrong (was it in the room with him?), but he was too tired to care, and passed into sleep.

*   *   *

In his dream, the world is on fire. He is walking down the middle of the street in his neighborhood, the apartment complex on one side, the middle class suburban houses on the other — they are all in flames. The blacktop is warm and soft under his feet and he has to keep moving in order to prevent the soft flesh of his soles from sizzling and burning. The air shimmers with threads of warmth. Many of the buildings stand now as dark, lifeless husks, their remains feeding the lively yellow flames. And there is something pressing in the back of his mind, something he needs to do, he thinks, as he peers through the melting window of a home he's not familiar with. And, as he watches, something throws itself at the window, breaking through, falling on the sidewalk. It looks to be a dog, the flames burning its fur, assaulting it like a colony of bright parasites. The dog tries to run, in a panic, passing him on the street, makes it a few yards, then collapses, its wails of pain cutting short: a smoke-wreathed lump of black.

And he hears other animals wailing, and they are running to either side of him, some with shiny open wounds; others still in flames. He sees dogs, and cats, and a black rabbit burned of all its hair. And he sees wilder beasts: a raccoon, a singed loping bear, an antelope with its grand rack of antlers like burnt, twisting tree branches. And then the horses come, galloping around him, some limping, others streaking by; whinnies and clopping hooves. All the animals are in a panic, running from something. They are making sounds; their screams sound human, like sick and wounded children.

He turns to see what they are running from. A pale, bald figure stands in the middle of the street at the crest of a hill, a silhouette against the violet sky. As he watches, the figure stoops down and moves forward on all-fours like an ape, its legs and arms pushing liquidly against the blacktop. It looks right at him and tries to smile, but its face sags, giving its eyes a crazed, bulging appearance.

Jake turns away and runs, but, as in a dream, his feet seem sluggish and slow. The tar sucks at the bottoms of his feet. He can feel the Melting Man gaining on him, closer and closer. He wills himself to wake up. The animals, all around him, are screaming.

And when he wakes he can still hear the screaming.

*   *   *

192

He sits up in bed, the sheets hot like just out of the dryer. He throws himself to his feet and stumbles across the room.

A movement, out of the corner of his eye — he turns just in time to see the gnome from earlier ducking behind the bed, crouching there, peering up at him. The hat the gnome wears looks ridiculous over his ugly, pock-marked face. The gnome grins, a mouthful of rotting yellow teeth, and disappears under his bed. He moves to go after the gnome — to see what the little guy wants this time — when the screaming changes pitch, becomes more desperate. Is that his mom? He turns away and crosses the room.

Opening the door, the heat nearly pushes him from his feet, flooding over him; it is stifling; the sweat instantly begins to dry sticky on his forehead and down the sides of his face. He pushes through the heat, down the hallway and the stairs. The living room is blazing, filled with curling hot swirls, mingling with the smoke into thick treacle draping across the room, the fire too large for the fireplace, spilling out, beginning to crawl up the walls and over a nearby sofa chair.

He stops, clutching his head as it throbs feverishly. The world spins — breathes, comes back into focus.

His mom screams again, which draws him forward. He takes a couple of steps, squinting to see through the haze. A wavering figure, his mom, is kneeling in the center of the living room, flailing her hands frantically.

As he approaches, he can see another figure — a crumpled mass — at her feet: his dad.

The TV flashes static into the room.

"Get out of here, Jake!"

Ignoring his mom, Jake continues, something inside of him driving him onward. It's the TV; there's a message in the squiggling snow, he just has to get close enough to see it.

He steps in front of the TV — ignoring the heat, and the smoke; ignoring the desperate pleas from his mom — and stares into the screen. And there is a pattern, something coming into focus, sorting itself out, approaching.

Jake takes a step back as he realizes — with complete terror — what is about to happen. He looks over at his mom, at his dad passed out on the floor. He's seen his dad's movie — he knows what happens next.

He stares into the screen, waiting for the elongated arm to snake out and grab him.

He will be possessed by the fiend within the television set. He will turn on his parents, with his new voice. He will use a knife to slice his dad's stomach open so that his dad falls to the floor, clutching his guts to keep them from sliding out. Then, he will laugh and turn on his mom.

In the movie, the house burns.

Jake raises his arms in anticipation. Something is forming in the writhing snow.

He waits.

Nothing happens.

Then, he can feel his mom's arms wrapping around him, pulling him away.

Then, a growl, and his world becomes a blur of motion. He doesn't really feel the blow, but hears it — a dull thud that sends dark sparks flying before his eyes — and he blinks, and the world goes black.

*   *   *

He blinked. The fire was all over the house now and he sees two figures struggling in the smoke. There was a dark smear on the hearth of the fireplace and he felt the hot blood running down the back of his head. Smoke clogged the air above him, obscuring the struggling figures to filmy blurs; only their feet were clearly visible.

He tried to focus. He heard the whoosh of flames hungrily snatching oxygen from the air, the snap of kindling, the pop of expanding heat. He tried to sit up, but the world flared in and out in a dizzying array of orange brightness.

He watched helplessly as his dad pushed his mom; she stumbled and fell with her back cracking against the couch; he heard her intake air with a hiss, and then she began to cough. His dad straddled her, pushing down against his mom's pitifully flailing arms, ignoring her choked screams, grinning gleefully.

This isn't real, Jake thought.

And then he saw his mother's face, turned to the side in the hot, flickering light, and the blood running down her cheek.

Jake's dad laughed and kicked Jake's mom in the stomach; he brought his foot back and kicked again. His mom doubled over helplessly. His dad brought his fist around and smashed his mom's nose to a shimmering pulp. His mom fell back and his dad kicked a third time. His mom made a sound, as if to vomit, and Jake saw the dark stain spreading rapidly between her legs, blooming through her skirt and beginning to pool over the floor.

"Stop," Jake said, his voice rough and burned.

"No more freak children," Jake's dad screamed in his mom's haggard face. He looked at Jake. "I'll get to you in a minute."

"Stop," Jake tried again, leaning up against the wall.

Jake's mom tried to stand and his dad kicked her back to the floor. His dad grinned as he brought the heel of his boot down on his mom's ribs, twisting and grinding. He spat in her hair. His mom coughed and writhed on the floor. His dad got down on one knee and threw a fist into her gut; his mom's trembling hands cupped her wounded belly; her legs convulsed. His dad stood over her, still grinning, and was now able to bring his boot down without his mom being able to move out of the way. His dad stomped once; twice, and another spot began to darken on the floor. His dad stomped once more, and then stood back, admiring his work; his blue jeans were spattered with blood.

Jack pushed himself to his feet.

He froze, his dad looking back at him again with those terrible dark-saucer eyes. "I said I'd get to you in a minute." His dad turned back to the motionless heap on the floor.

Jake staggered across the living room. He had to get help; he had to call somebody. But he couldn't see: his eyes burned and watered; every breath was like inhaling sand. The house was a furnace, unbearably hot. The living room was thick with smoke and crossing it was like parting a liquid veil. He pushed toward the front door.

"Where do you think you're going?" his dad growled, right behind him.

Jake crossed to the door, flailing his arms out for the doorknob. He couldn't breathe; he was holding his breath. His heart yammered painfully in his chest. His fingers brushed the knob; he grasped it; it began to turn.

Something heavy and hot fell on his shoulder. He was spun around, violently, and found himself staring into those dark smoldering eyes, framed against the living room walls splattered with dancing fire. His dad's breath — meat rotting in the sun — smothered him in a hot cloud.

"I need you to do something for me, son," his dad said. "I need your help."

Jake struggled, but his dad's grip was firm.

"You're special. You're the only one who can help."

Jake could hardly breathe. He felt his consciousness wavering. The words came out of his mouth, "What do you need me to do?"

His dad's grin widened grotesquely. "Come with me."

An explosion filled the living room with a white flashing light — the television had fallen to the floor, its life sputtering away on the floor. His dad's grip on his shoulders loosened for a moment and Jake tore himself free. He grappled with the doorknob and flung the door wide. He ran out into the front yard. He turned: the entire house was on fire; he could feel its heat pushing on his face. For a moment, he watched the flames, parading over the structure where he'd spent much of his childhood, eating it from the inside out; a couple of gnomes jeered from the upper story windows; one of them waved a flaming log in its hand, waving it as if to say goodbye. Then, his dad was in the doorway.

"Son! Get back here!"

Jake ran down the street, as fast as he could, heading in the familiar direction, towards his school, and Sherwood Forest.

TWENTY-SEVEN

He was halfway to his school before he could begin to think. He should have stopped at the first possible house to bang on the door and demand help, he realized, but he hadn't. The morning light was just beginning to open the night sky, still too early for anyone to be about.

He was running and his dad was following; when he risked a glance over his shoulder, he could see him back there, limping slightly with each loping stride, coming after him, not quickly, but always there, showing no signs of slowing. And now he'd entered the edge of the neighborhood, the section where the money had run out and development had ceased; the section where the houses became empty half-built husks interspersed with vacant weed-encrusted lots. He'd find no help here. The world had gone bad. And he was at the end of it.

He turned, and dashed across the empty street. He took a shortcut he knew along the edge of the apartment complex, down to the path that skirted the drainage creek. For the moment, his dad was lost to sight behind the buildings. He felt woozy, his head throbbing, his legs growing heavy and sluggish, but he pressed on.

He came upon the concrete drainage pipe where he'd seen the weird thing with a face, and began to climb down. The rocks were slick with phosphorous algae, but this was one of the only ways down directly from the bike path. His hand slipped and he caught himself on his shoulder. He forced himself not to rush, to take his time. The opening into the dark tunnel beneath the city loomed over him. He eased himself down onto a small ledge, careful not to drop his foot into an adjacent crystal pool. In his mind he saw his dad stepping up on top of the pipe, his shadow casting over the side, grinning down at him. He made one final jump, and his feet sank into the moist sand. He looked behind him—no sign of his dad. He padded out into the middle of the open creek bed and looked again: no sign of movement or sound; he was alone.

He began to make his way downstream. He noticed marks in the sand. He followed them to a spot where the firm sand became moist and soft and he was better able to make out what the markings were. After that, he followed the footprints.

His pace had slowed considerably through the haze of his throbbing head, but every time he looked behind him, he was alone still. His path took him threading amongst the swampy frog pools, then up through the grassy hillocks. He followed the dusty inlaid path up and over each rise, the footprints strangely familiar; the path strangely familiar. He came to the edge of Sherwood Forest, took one last look behind him—nothing but the open expanse of the creek, the rivulets like cracks in the earth's crust, the sky a dim gray cathedral ceiling—and plunged through the foliage and into the cover of shadows.

Inside was the small and familiar grove, the organic smell of earth, the gentle breeze through the rattling tree leaves. The chunks of wood he'd nailed to the side of a nearby tree like rungs on a ladder climbed up to the platforms of scrap wood he'd used to make his tree house. In here, the trail of footprints he'd been following were lost in the swirl of scuffs in the dirt. He walked to the middle of the grove and stood for a moment. Now what? What was he doing here?

For a moment, a veil fell over the world and he swooned. He fought to keep his feet. He brought his hand to the back of his head and gingerly applied pressure with his fingers; the bleeding had stopped, but he was soft and sore.

He looked around. The footprints resumed at the far edge of the grove, almost invisible beneath the bough of a sagging branch. He was on a course now; he knew where he was intended to go, as if he'd stumbled into a dream. He pushed the branch out of the way and there was another path, thin and winding, hardly visible amongst the encroaching growth. He began to push his way along it.

After some time, the path came out upon a small barren patch of earth at the base of a massive tree.

The tree was ancient and leafless, perhaps dead from long ago, its branches snaking upwards and around through the denseness of the live foliage. There was a hole at the base of the tree and he knew this was where he was supposed to go; the footprints walked down the loamy slope and disappeared into the darkness.

For the first time, he hesitated. What was he really doing here? A spray of fear speckled his heart, began to spread like ink over a wet scrap of cloth, blooming in threads. The dark hole in the tree seemed to beckon like a mouth, eager to have him, to chew him up. He remembered something his dad had told him once: "The world is a funny place, Jake. People lie; they'll manipulate you if they get half a chance. You have to be careful of what's out there. If you're ever unsure of something, stop what you're doing and think about it. Then, if it still seems like the right thing to do, go on ahead, but don't ever let yourself be tricked into doing something you don't really want to do."

Jake smiled, thinking about dad, his *sober* dad, his *real* dad. He looked at the tree, at the footprints leading down into that dark crevasse. He began to turn back.

There was a crashing and snapping sound coming down the narrow path towards him, closer and closer, louder and louder. His dad's face appeared above the leaves, looked at him. For a moment, his dad's face was a slack blankness, eyes empty of inflection, then they clouded with milky squiggles and the drooping lips rose into that grin. "There you are, son. I'm coming for you!"

The malice in that voice was too much; Jake stumbled down the loamy incline and ran in the only direction he had left: he dropped to his knees and wriggled into the darkness.

Inside, his hands and knees sunk several inches into soft mud. He clambered onward, as fast as he could, ignoring the sickening squelch pushing between his fingers, moving blindly at first; then, as his eyes slowly adjusted to the dimness, he could make out the outlines of a tunnel, burrowing through the earth. The smell was rancid, nearly unbearable at first—he retched, even as he moved—like bread left to decay into a fungal jelly, or the split remains of necrotic intestines open in a fetid pool—but his nose soon adjusted to the smell, the acidic panic pumping through him overruling all other senses.

"I'm right behind you."

The light from the tunnel opening cut out and Jake knew his dad had crawled inside and was coming after him.

"Keep going. I'm right behind you."

Jake pushed on, leaving the light from the outside behind him completely and coming into another sort of light, a yellowing glow. And as he crawled, the light—only subtly, but noticeably—began to intensify. The tunnel continued into darkness, but to his right there was an opening and it was from this opening the light was coming from, so he took it, sliding down and sloshing to a stop in another tunnel. He stood; this tunnel much larger than the last. He had two choices: the tunnel branched to the right or left; both looked equally dim and unappealing. He took a step to the right, but something snagged in his brain. He knew the tunnel to the right was a dead end: it led to a door, a locked door; he'd dreamed of it, he must have. He took the left tunnel and began to run, his feet slapping at the mud.

The tunnel was winding, sometimes going right, then turning left, but the ground was relatively level and the tunnel remained a uniform width, always creeping steadily downward, down into the deep. He ran and ran, losing track of time, his mind blank, his lungs burning the moist air.

He could no longer hear his dad shouting behind him. His dad must be struggling to get his bulk through the tunnel, or he'd fallen quiet in order to sneak up on him.

The tunnel came to another carved opening, an arching doorway hung with filth. He staggered through the doorway and into a large circular chamber filled with that yellowish light. A tower of junk, woven into a spiraling column, sat at its center. Looking up, Jake lost sight of its reaches, the warm lighting blinding him; he could just make out the wisps of a few low-hanging clouds.

Jake looked behind him; his dad was back there somewhere; he didn't know how much time he had. He wondered what was on the other side of the junk pile, if there was another tunnel, farther reaches to flee into.

He took a few steps into the room; hesitated. A rustling sound came from within the construct of detritus; a door was flung open about two stories up; a head emerged.

"You made it! Excellent!"

The figure slid forward from the open door and took his seat upon his chair. The chair swung from lashing that twisted upwards into the construct; a large lampshade hung over the chair cast a pall over the hairless and emaciated creature, further leeching his skin of pigment to a gray colorlessness that seemed to deny even the shadows a crevasse to rest in.

"I knew you'd come," the Melting Man said.

Jake didn't know what to do next. "You did?"

"Oh yes. You've come to help me, just as you promised you would." The creature's head stretched out, its neck an elongated limb. "You've come to free me from this prison. You're quite an individual; if you only knew...An accident, really, but a fortunate one." The creature grinned and Jake found that grin disturbingly familiar.

The Melting Man leaned back in his chair; the ropes groaned under his weight. "There aren't many of us left, you know. Only a few—banished to this nether-world or the next, playing what subtle parts we still can in The Grand Masquerade; it's all we have left. But you..."

"What about me?"

The Melting Man's large eyes glimmered with excitement. "You can open the gate. We can go home."

Jake looked at the Melting Man swinging in his chair; he didn't trust that grin. "Why should I?"

"What?" the Melting Man said, leaning forward. "What was that?"

He tried again, "Why should I?"

The Melting Man recoiled, falling back melodramatically, as if slapped, and nearly toppled from his perch, the chair swinging wildly. For a moment he resembled something lost and forlorn, holding on desperately until the chair began to settle.

The Melting Man hung his head. "You'd not help me? There is so much you don't understand. I had hoped..."

"Who are you?"

The Melting Man's grin returned; he raised his head, liquid eyes swimming with mischief. "You may call me ZimZim; it's as good a name as any."

Jake felt the blood leap through his veins, pounding hotly in his head. He could feel himself growing lighter, as if his feet had left the ground. He blinked, forced himself to focus, not to pass out, "And where did you come from?"

"Ah. That is a story. A long story. Unfortunately, I fear, we may not have time for such idle banter."

Behind him, Jake heard grunting. He turned to see his dad bursting through the opening. His dad looked terrible: raw unshaven skin, greasy yellow nose, ragged hair, black-pitted eyes sunk into purple bruises drifting with whitish murk like cataracts. His skin was creased and twisted with wrinkles, as if by some great stress or internal struggle, churning just beneath the surface.

Jake staggered back.

"There...You...Are..." His dad choked on the words, lifting his hands up like claws, reaching towards him.

The world swooned; his vision fogged; he began to lose consciousness.

TWENTY-EIGHT

He saw his dad moving towards him even as he was passing away into the fizzing darkness. He felt his dad's hands padding over him, and then settle around his neck. The air was instantly cut from his lungs.

He awoke, suddenly, for a moment, to look into his dad's greasy face. The air whistled feverishly in and out of his dad's nose and mouth and his dad's eyes remained dark, milky swirled hollows, then cleared for a second, just as Jake's eyes fluttered, grew heavy, and began to sag closed.

"No. Please," he heard his dad mumbling. The grip around his neck loosened the tiniest bit.

"That's enough," the Melting Man called down from his throne.

Instantly, his neck was free, and Jake fell sinking into the mud, gasping for air, dark sparkles cascading through his vision like nightmare fireworks.

*   *   *

When he'd recovered enough to lift his head, he looked up, saw his dad had backed away from him and was leaning up against the wall by the entrance. His dad looked strangely casual, patient even.

He lifted his head farther, to peer up at the Melting Man, whose pale, stretched face watched him with a mix of curiosity, amusement, and concern.

"How do you feel?" the Melting Man inquired.

Jake struggled with his words, running up his throat like sandpaper. "Not good," he said.

"Please. Catch your breath."

Jake sat in the filth. Slowly, his vision began to clear. As he looked about, he could see the shapes of things mired in the mud. Nearby, he spotted an old manila rotary phone, cracked and stained. A few feet away, there was one rusty side of an old pair of pruning shears and, next to it, a frying pan, newer-looking, like the one his mom used to fry eggs.

Jake glanced at his dad, then up at the Melting Man again. "Did you say your name was ZimZim?"

The Melting Man's grin was like a slice through raw dough. "Yes. I did."

Jake's mind reeled, trying to come to grips with the implications of this new-found knowledge.

"I think we have time now. Shall I tell you my story?"

Jake stammered, unable to coax a response from his throat.

"Excellent," the Melting Man said as if Jake's choking and coughing was a sign of vigorous interest. "As I told you before, I am now forbidden from setting foot on the grounds of this place, but once, I was its keeper. Yes, that's right. I was appointed to this hellhole, and, at the time, glad to have the position, honored even." He shook his glistening head sadly. "I was chosen because I was crafty, or so I thought, and the most skilled amongst my kind; no one could take it from me." A white slug tongue ran out over his lips, flashing pale toothless gums. "I was his favorite," he hissed.

Jake watched this strange creature with interest. In many ways he was closer, more intimate, with this forlorn figure — with ZimZim — than he was with his parents.

"So," the Melting Man continued, "I was trapped here by my master. I was appointed Gatekeeper, and, for a time, I was useful. 'Guard each gate carefully,' my master told me. 'The smallest of leaks — organism, chemical, atmosphere, or energy — from any one world to the next can be catastrophic. Only one gate may ever be open at a time and you must never let anything through.' It was only many years later, as I sat alone and forsaken in my own filth, that I thought to question my master, and the possible harm he might be causing, passing from one world to the next. I was naive."

Jake looked at his dad: still leaning against the wall, blank, no expression, staring straight ahead. So strange; why didn't his dad do something?

"At the beginning, my master appeared frequently, always with an air of importance, his gray robes fluttering out behind him as he stalked through the halls. Sometimes he even stayed for a while, sharing

with me the things he'd seen and the projects he'd
been working on. At the time I was enamored by his
influence and his power. I was blind to what he really
was."

The Melting Man paused, kicking his feet lightly
so that his chair rocked gently back and forth. He
wrung his hands together, round eyes looking distantly into the past.

Jake crossed his legs and leaned back on his hands
so that he could more comfortably stare at the Melting Man and listen. His rapidly beating heart was
beginning to settle. He could think of nothing else
to do. The unreality of the situation buoyed him com-
fortingly, as if upon a warm sea.

"I don't know how he came to know so much,
what pacts he made with what sordid deities, but I've
never seen the likes of such powers since. His archi-
tectural skills were incredible. How he designed this
place, what labor he must have employed to build it,
I can only wonder at."

Jake looked about at the earthen walls, thought
about the dark earthworm tunnels he'd clamored
through, looked up at the skyscraper of junk, at the
dark churning mess surrounding him that he'd become a part of, and wondered what ZimZim was
talking about.

"I know what you're thinking," the Melting Man
said. "This place doesn't look like much, not now.
But you don't understand. You should have seen it!"
His smile stretched lazily from one side of his face to
the other.

"For a while, my master's visits were frequent and
fairly regular. He came casually sometimes, seeming

to pick one of the gates at random, disappearing for a couple of hours only to appear again later to try another. In the beginning it had been serious business, but by then it had become a sort of game; he didn't seem to care what I did or why I did it.

"One day I asked him—after an unusually long period of absence, his visits becoming more and more infrequent, each more hurried than the last—if there was any way, if I was no longer needed, I could return home. I remember perfectly what he said: 'It's impossible to say when you will no longer be needed. My machines have changed everything.' He looked very tired as he spoke these words. When I pushed him for a more specific answer he said, 'Yes, yes, I'll see what I can do,' waved his hand to dismiss me, and flung himself through the nearest gate.

"I did not see him after that, not for a long while. I tried to count the days, at first, but they became jumbled, each meaningless space of minutes and hours blended into the next, until a time had passed that was incomprehensible to me. As days crept into months and months into years I began to forget myself. I lived; I existed, but for what purpose? I ate when I was hungry and I slept when I was tired. I forsook my cleaning and organizational duties and things began to pile; I began to horde the worthless dreck that came to me from the portal above this chamber." His eyes slid upwards and he pointed up the winding junk pile that was his home. "And, as conditions worsened, I began to eat only when I found something, like a scavenger; like a drug addict I wallowed about in the growing mess, and I began to forget where I came from and who I was.

I considered suicide—I could have hung myself easily enough, even designed and built my own gallows in preparation, but I clung to my master's words, his promise to send me home when I was no longer needed." The chair creaked on its ropes as the Melting Man moved to the convictions of his story.

"I waited and I waited, until I no longer knew if ten years had passed or a thousand. I was trapped in my own hell, in a purgatorial numbness. How long I lived like this, it is impossible for me to comprehend. I could not open the gates—they had been sealed from me from the beginning—but I knew the one that would return me home. I sat for long hours before it in a fugue of despair and longing.

"Then, one day, I found a curious device, strewn amongst the various other random objects that scattered the floor of this chamber. It was long and cylindrical and, at the pushing of a button, produced an orange beam of light from one end. The light was similar to that which illuminated these halls, and, for the first time, I began to consider the mechanism behind my master's creations. By that time, more than half of the hot glowing lights had gone dark, like lifeless eyeballs, but I'd not thought to be concerned by this. The hand-held light I'd found burnt for a minute or two more, then joined the others in darkness."

The Melting Man fell silent for a moment, lost in remembrance. Jake watched him, enrapt in the story of this curious creature, unconcerned with anything else. The Melting Man hung his head in concentration, rocking in his chair. Minutes passed. After a while, the Melting Man lifted his head, and continued:

"I began to think more after that, questions began to well up in my brain, things I'd not considered, things repressed. I was ignorant; I can admit that now. I'd thought, without knowing it, that my master was infallible. I'd assumed my master knew better than I, but did he? He'd treated this place like a television studio, each gate like a show, setup for his amusement, whimsical distractions for him to play around with. He failed to consider or care what irreparable damage he might be causing to the individuals in these worlds. I had looked up to him like a god! I had followed his edicts blindly and never once thought to question his wisdom.

"Sitting there, holding the flashlight—as I was to later learn it was called—I was forced to imagine what it would be like in this place without light. Oh, what torment! Without sight, what could I do? How could I live?

"If the light could fail—the light provided by my master—what else might cease to be provided? What if the food stopped coming from above? What if it grew cold? What could I do? I cursed my master's name and, in a moment of anger, snatched my excrement from the floor and flung it at the nearest gate. It splattered, and stuck."

The Melting Man paused. Jake wrinkled his nose and looked around. He looked at the muddy walls, at the items mired in the smear. He pulled his hands from the muck and held them out, staring at them in partial disbelief and disgust.

The Melting Man was nodding his head. "Yes. That's right. One secretes much over a thousand years. You see, I had grown terrified I might not be able to find the door back home in the total dark, and I was appalled by this place, by its horrid violation of the natural way of things — I imagined it like a tumor, a dark, twisting growth, leaking poison into the ethereal structure — so I began to cover it. I don't know how long it took, but it felt natural, the right thing to do. I covered the walls and the floors and, using an old chair as a step stool, even the ceiling. I covered each and every gate, all of them, that is, except for one.

"I also, around that time, began to search the rubbish more thoroughly, looking for anything useful. I began to organize things again, mostly by size and type. I began to study what I found and experiment, learning what I could from these seemingly random objects, to wonder where they came from. I turned from supplicant follower to archaeologist: I wanted to know more about a people capable of producing so many intricate things, only to lose them, or throw them away while they still had function. Many of the things I found were alien to me; it took long hours to uncover their secrets, and it was, by chance, that I discovered a pair of cylindrical objects that seemed to match the size and shape of those within the flashlight. I took the existing columns out and replaced them with those that I had found and, to my astonishment, the light burned again. I had found a source of power, and, I reasoned, if it could power the flashlight, it could surely power other things as well.

"You see, I had all the time in the world; years upon years to experiment and teach myself to harness the bits and pieces that daily dumped into my little corner of existence, my prison. I taught myself to build things. I made lights and heat sources that did not burn with fire. And, eventually, I salvaged a small generator, that I slowly improved and built upon, that consumed a raw black sludge I filtered into it. You can hear it humming now."

Jake cocked his head, and yes, he could hear it: a low, ever-present rumbling.

"Then, one day, as I was laying out my most recent finds, my Master burst into the chamber, coming from nowhere, as if he'd not been gone all that time. He was very angry, I could tell immediately. 'You disgusting creature,' he cried. 'What have you done?'

"At first I didn't know what he meant. I crouched on the floor and looked at my Master, not saying a word—had I once revered this being? His robes drooped, his boots were caked with excrement, his beard was threadbare and the wrinkles about his eyes made him old. He held his hand out, in the old way, to show his dominance over me, as if I were a wild dog, as if he meant to smack me on the head in punishment for what I'd done, but I only stared back, unmoving.

"'You have defiled my chamber. You have forsaken the task that was appointed to you and you alone, above all others whom would have gladly given their lives for a chance to be in your position.' His robes flickered. 'I came only as a courtesy to you, to let you know you can never return home. I came to give you my condolences, that your world has been overrun. But now I see this!' He waved at the excrement covered walls.

"My Master moved forward, his palm still out to me, and I hated Him. I wasn't really listening. I knew he was lying to me. He had kept me here as a prisoner, away from contact with other beings as a way to deny me The Masquerade, as he had done with the rest of my people, convincing us to follow him blindly, that he could provide a better life for us, but I knew him for what he was: The Father of Lies. I lashed out like an animal. I'd been alone so long I didn't know how else to express my anger. A deep growl escaped my throat.

"'Don't snap at me, you cur,' my Master said, pulling his hand back quickly. 'I'll not set such a beast on this world or the next.' He turned then, and strode to the doorway. 'I forbid you access to my chamber.' He drew a sigil in the air. 'You will live here only by the trash of other worlds, never to set foot upon the floors of my creation.'

The Melting Man stopped. His face was running with a deep sadness. "I've lived here ever since, in this scrap heap, biding my time. I've not seen my Master since."

Jake watched the Melting Man's face with curiosity; it seemed his eyes themselves might glob and begin to run down his cheeks.

After several minutes, the Melting Man's face lifted. "But you wouldn't believe what wonders I've built, even from the confines of this dwelling." His eyes met Jake's. "I have my own lights now. I've been able to watch your world from glowing television screens installed within this structure, run on the power from my generator, even communicate with others of my kind."

Jake lifted his head, lolling heavily upon his shoulders. "There are others? Others like you?"

The Melting Man grinned. "Yes, of course there are. I've had help from my brothers and sisters in The Masquerade. It began with the videos sent to your father. I thought I could reach you through him, but, instead of going himself to find the video makers, he sent his bitch girlfriend to do his dirty work for him. So, I used that fool Trevor again, but your mother never really warmed to him like I would have liked. It would have been so much easier if I could have reached you directly, but that's simply not possible."

Jake was confused. "Why not? What's The Masquerade?"

"Yes, yes. I was getting to that. I don't expect you to understand, but my people have been an integral part of history in your world and others. Physically, we're very fragile, but in our native element...Ah, to be home, to be floating amongst my kindred beings—looking out, the vast fields of purple and blue stretching for miles; mists of the deepest green grow about pools of amber luminescence; floating in peace, watching the comets passing before the darkened sky..." He paused. "I'm sorry. I'm at a loss for words. It's like a dream to me now. We guide other species, help them to grow strong."

"I don't understand."

"That's fine. You needn't. But now you know my torment!" The Melting Man leaned forward, the chair tilting dangerously, the ropes creaking. "I'm trapped. I need you to open the door so I can go home. So *we* can go home. You have a piece of me within you, after all."

"A piece of *you*?"

"Yes, of course." The Melting Man stared over

Jake's shoulders with intense liquid eyes; they darkened.

Jake jumped at his dad's voice: "I was with your father, your real father — that Trevor idiot — when you were conceived," his dad said hoarsely. Jake turned in time to see that grin stretch his dad's face, then drop, his dad slumping back against the wall, staring blankly. Jake turned back to see that grin on the Melting Man's face.

"Do you get it now?"

Jake stared at the Melting Man, then back at his dad. "This is a dream."

"Is that a question? I'll not tell you otherwise. Is this really happening? Surely. It must be. But perhaps that's not what's important. What is real and what isn't is a matter of relative perception, wouldn't you say? What can be made real — that's what matters. How do you think things came to be this way in the first place? Someone had to imagine them into existence."

Jake's heart was beginning to race again. He felt his face growing hot. "You were controlling my dad."

"Yes. I was."

"But I thought you needed my help? You killed my mom! You almost killed me!"

The Melting Man looked at him, didn't seem to understand his anger. "Yes?"

"How can you expect me to help you after all that?" He was starting to really wake up now. "You're a — a piece of shit, that's what you are. I'd never help you. I hate you!"

"I *was* upset with you — I'll admit that. You kept avoiding me and I wasn't very happy. But you still don't get it, do you, my son? It's a part of the game, a part of the story. It's for the drama: for The Masquerade. Your parents are just pieces on the game board. They're pawns and you're the king, Jake. As soon as you realize this fact, the better off you'll be. But don't worry; I'll help you to understand."

"Fuck you."

"Don't be angry. Perhaps I didn't explain myself well enough. You see…"

"Fuck you!"

The Melting Man looked sad again. "Did you really think your life belonged to you? I didn't want to have to use force. I thought you'd understand."

Jake stood, his fists clenched at his sides. How could he understand?

The Melting Man clapped his hands together. "Lympha," he called. "You can come out now."

Jake's eyes were drawn to a noise at the bottom of the junk castle, to a large armoire, its closed doors beginning to rattle.

"You see," the Melting Man continued, "you were an accident—my progeny—given powers I once had, before I relinquished them to my Master." Something wet was flopping against the doors, the latch squealing as it was pulled from the wood. "I decided to try something. I thought, if you were given powers from me, perhaps I could create my own being with powers taken from you." The wet flop thumped the door again, the latch screamed.

"So, I took your seed."

The latch ripped free and the doors shattered open.

"The results, unfortunately, were less than successful."

Jake's mind whirred. That dream. The wet dream. The one where he'd awoken, his stomach wet and sticky.

Something large and soggy struggled to drag itself forward, its skin pale and writhing like a grub.

TWENTY-NINE

The thing that moved towards him was large and unreal.

How long had he been dreaming?

He fought to control the visions of events past spinning through his head like a maelstrom, to organize them chronologically, to put them into separate columns of fact and fiction. There was the fire at the house; his parents had been acting weird and he'd fallen asleep in his bedroom upstairs and everything after that must be a dream: the house on fire; his dad kicking his mom; running through the empty neighborhood at dawn. Or, perhaps, when he'd hit his head on the fireplace or passed out from the smoke. Things had progressed strangely after that. Or farther back; he was asleep at school, at his desk: the fire, his parents fight, the ancient tree and its dark tunnels; none of it, or any of the weird things he'd seen on his walks to and from school. Surely this couldn't be happening: The Melting Man's crazy story, and now this thing before him. None of it.

It pawed forward on unequal wads at the end of malformed limbs.

The Melting Man continued to talk: "Did you like my story? I enjoy telling stories. It's nice to have someone to tell them to, after all this time."

It moved slowly, dragging much of its anatomy as if it'd been turned inside out. As it loomed closer, Jake was forced to witness its struggles, its smell — sour milk curdling amongst its putrid folds of flesh — overpowering. Its skin, or what resembled skin, was gray and translucent, clots of fat wriggled visibly about inside it. It was a baby, although huge, its head bald and smooth, too heavy for its neck, dragging behind it, along with organs that might have been its bowels and stomach, through the muck. Other organs were visible as well, that seemed to have no other function than to gurgle and wheeze, dripping fluids, leaving a trail of something like pus. Its eyes were white and glazed like something out of the deep sea, and only one seemed capable of sight, glued in Jake's direction. And yes, there was a resemblance; Jake could see, although not a close likeness, certain kindred features, a parody of him, of what he might have become raised in a nightmare. It appalled him. He began to back away.

But he was already too late. It liquefied up to him; he had nowhere left to go, backed against the chamber wall. It pressed against him.

The Melting Man continued to talk, but Jake was no longer listening.

Its face lolled within the soft shell of its skull. Its eye—holding a baby's single-minded hunger—remained fixed on him, unblinking so as not to miss a moment of his panic. Its mouth yawned: dribbling toothless gums; a dark maw of hot rotting breath. It tried to push its head forward in the hopes he might fall down its muggy throat, but Jake pushed back into the wall, sinking into the excrement. An insanely normal human arm whipped forward, the fingers of its hand grown to twice their normal length beginning to dig at the soft wall.

"I didn't have any milk, you see," the Melting Man was saying, "so I nursed her on blood…"

Jake wriggled back into the softness, desperate to escape. The hand ripped into the filth. The wall of excrement cracked, dislodging a jagged clump that fell heavily by his side. Jake dropped to the ground and flopped, clawing his way forward. He felt the hand snatch at him, then slide away. He risked a glance as he struggled in the muck. An entire section of the wall had come down, eroding into a dark drift. Jake could see the makings of a door, and part of another.

Lympha lunged towards him and shrieked; a string of her dangling entrails was caught beneath the rubble, her face slumped within her bulbous head, coming forward for a moment, fish eye rolling, then sinking back, losing substance to the gelatinous.

Jake took the opportunity to scramble backwards. He watched, fascinated, as Lympha tried to tear herself free. The beast thrashed, rolling her head back and forth like a grindstone, its mutant fist coming down like a mallet, over and over against the floor. The chamber shook with her efforts. Jake could hear

ZimZim laughing loon-like above him. Then, there was a sound, like ripping fabric, and Lympha gave off a strangely babyish, yet deafening, wail. The entire monstrous body jerked forward and slumped, eye spinning wildly. Its thrashings ceased for a moment, and it lay still.

Above him, the Melting Man continued to cackle. The twang of snapping rope, and a crash.

Jake turned, looking up, but the Melting Man was gone, a flayed strand of rope bobbing where the chair had been. The chair was caught in the rubble a part of the way down. A pale, crumpled form lifted himself, slick with his own excrement, and stared at him.

The Melting Man looked around, held his hands out to examine them. "I'm...I'm okay."

"I thought you were forbidden to set foot in this place?" Jake said.

Slowly, the Melting Man's grin began to return. "I was."

"How much of your story is actually true?"

"All of it. In a way."

That wasn't really an answer and Jake was about to say so when something stirred behind him.

Lympha was awake. She groaned and wriggled.

"Now what?" Jake said.

"Now you do what I say or your father dies."

Before Jake could react, Lympha's elongated arm shot out and snatched his dad—who'd been leaning this entire time against the wall like a discarded mannequin—in her grimy fingers and swung him up like a limp rag.

Jake jumped forward, not sure what he intended to do. The point of something jutted from the ground and he bent to pull it free. He held one half of an ancient pair of pruning shears by its moldering wooden handle. Without thinking, he lunged. He aimed for that hateful eye. He felt the rusty spike thump into something, then it was wrenched from his hands, and he was thrown to the ground.

Lympha seethed, rocking her head back and forth, but was otherwise unconcerned with the spike that now protruded from her skull several inches just above her tiny liquid eye.

Jake cast around for another weapon.

"Don't," the Melting Man said.

Jake looked up and Lympha had folded his dad into her mouth and was gumming him sloppily.

"I can make him suffer."

As Jake watched, his dad's face emerged from the goop; did he see pleading in his dad's eyes? "Fine," Jake said. "I'll help you if that's what you really want. Just leave us alone after that."

Jake turned, throwing his arms down, and his gaze met with the Melting Man's. "Of course," the Melting Man said. "Shall we go then?" He indicated the doorway with a white hand that appeared only partially formed.

When the Melting Man didn't move right away, Jake took the first step forward. He was eager to get this over with, but the Melting Man seemed determined to take his time. They walked side by side and Jake had to keep looking over his shoulder to be sure Lympha continued to follow them—dragging her head and body laboriously—with his dad. They moved through the doorway and began down the long hallway.

As they walked, he couldn't help but look at the strange creature beside him; he'd never seen the Melting Man this close. He was very small, shorter than Jake. And his manila skin was stretched and shiny in some places, and bunched and folded in others. He limped along, as if one leg were longer than the other. And his face — his face that was too large for his skull; that mouth that seemed to split his head in half; those eyes that crowded his forehead, wet and wavering and unblinking, pulsing almost rhythmically as they grew and shrank to different diameters at different times. He was nose-less and hairless. He wore nothing for clothing and had no discernible genitalia, his feet sinking and expanding as they flopped along.

After a minute or two, the Melting Man spoke. "It's funny how things turn out, don't you think? How they mold and shift. How one struggle for reality and purpose comes up against another, shifting into something neither one could have predicted or expected."

Jake said nothing.

"I watched your people, my son, for many long years. Before my Master brought me here, I played my part in The Masquerade, but I never met such a large group of beings so polarized by a single deity."

Jake watched the Melting Man lick his lips with a tongue long enough to snake up and over his eyes, wetting them.

"Your people spend hours and hours in supplication, in reverence before it, praying, learning from its teachings, letting it absorb into you, forming a social power of common beliefs and dreams, each of you striving to be whatever Television — your preacher, your god — says you should be. It's incredible."

"What? TV?" Jake shook his head. "TV's not our god."

"Is it not?"

"No way."

"You're too young to understand, son. But you will. One day. It's certainly a tool of control; I'm sure of that." The Melting Man wore a sly smile. He stopped. "We're here."

The door was not large, but seemed to lean towards them, as if beckoning Jake to open it.

The scowl Jake had been wearing deepened. "So what's on the other side?"

"Rolling fields, blanketed with flowering foliage, all manner of colors; the deep golden pools of my people glowing with vibrancy and importance; the cloudless sky like a green marble dome. And, perhaps, the Jollas will be out this time of year, slithering upon tentacles like writhing bushels of snakes, their pointed beaks herding insects into the open, barking, scooping up the crunchy morsels before scuttling back into the brush. And my kindred, wandering about — those not meditating in the pools, enmeshed in The Masquerade — basking in the luxury of time to consider the nature of existence. You'd like it, Jake. You'd be the only one of your kind, but you'd like it, I'm sure of that."

Jake looked back. Lympha had stopped a few feet behind them — she still held his dad in her gums.

"Well?" the Melting Man coaxed. "Open it."

Jake hesitated. "And then you'll let my dad go?"

The Melting Man's eyes were huge black pits. "Yes…"

Jake took a step forward. He grasped the knob, turned it, and pushed. The door didn't budge.

"Not like that. Your muscles are no use here. Concentrate."

Jake didn't know what the Melting Man meant, but clearly he was supposed to open the door with his mind, or his spirit—something like that. He dropped his eyes to his feet. If this was a dream, he felt he must wake soon.

"Oh, yes."

There was a rush of sucking air, and a blast of muggy heat enveloped him and the Melting Man. When Jake looked up—astonished—the door was gone. At first he could see nothing. Then, slowly, a field of black revealed itself.

"Finally," the Melting Man breathed, and Jake had to move to the side as the Melting Man stepped up to the door, his eyes glazed with wonder, his oversized mouth hanging open in a slack-jawed grin.

The Melting Man stepped across the threshold, and began down a hill of dark, quivering weeds. The Melting Man was a pale floating figure against the darkness. The sky was a spilled inky black.

Jake turned and realized his dad was still swimming within Lympha's fluid maw. "Wait…" he began, torn between calling after the Melting Man and going to his dad. But Lympha was still, seemed to have fallen asleep, the wheezing and blubbering of her organs slowed to a calm steadiness. And his dad was staring at him, trapped between those slimy pink gums like a vise, his legs visible as translucent stumps through Lympha's gelatinous skin, his head just clear, jutting outward, eyes aware with a mix of bewilderment and terror. His dad mouthed something.

Jake approached the shuddering creature slowly, trying to make out what his dad was attempting to say to him. Within only a few feet, his dad tried again, but saliva-pus was oozing down over his dad's face, obscuring his mouth to a wavering reflection.

Jake shuffled closer, careful not to make any noise. He looked at his dad.

Something shot forward, with a speed he'd not thought such a creature capable of, and snatched him around the waist. Lympha's hand lifted him, and squeezed painfully.

"Help! Jake!" His dad's scream was muffled, but audible. "You don't have to do anything that fuck tells you to."

Jake wiggled and thrashed, trying to free himself, but Lympha's grip was absolute. Lympha's eyelids opened, one after the other, and that eye slid up to stare at him with a desperate hate; that eye, flooded with accusation, blaming him for giving it this painful and unnatural life. The many-jointed fingers constricted; Jake could feel his bones bending and grinding against each other; his innards lurched upwards into his chest and throat. One look at that eye and Jake knew Lympha's intention: patricide.

His hands flailed. He began to see spots of inverted dark matter closing in around his vision. His lungs were crushed; he couldn't draw breath. His hand brushed against something hard and cold. Instinct wrapped his fingers around it and pulled.

Something popped. Hot stickiness gushed over him. He thrashed in the sickening jelly. Greasy strings of matter flowed from a wound in Lympha's head, like curdling mayonnaise from a pressurized balloon. He sunk to the ground and watched in awe as Lympha's life poured out of her, mingling with the surrounding filth. Her eye was already glazed, sightless as a dead fish.

Jake went to his dad—who was pulling himself free of the anatomical tangle—still gripping the handle of the broken half of the pruning shears he'd pulled free. "Dad…" He threw himself into his dad's arms.

He pictured wildly all those times his dad had sat by the side of his bed, lovingly reading him stories from books, sometimes making them up, until he fell asleep.

"Jake, thank God," his dad said—and it really *was* his dad, not the drunk and angry ZimZim puppet—and they gripped each other tight.

They lost themselves in each other's arms for who knew how long, ignoring the shit around them; Jake felt surging, relieving warmth inside him, never wanted it to end.

After a while, Jake lifted his head from his dad's shoulder. The doorway remained open. Maybe he could close it. He walked up to the opening, slowly, pulling his dad by the hand alongside him, unwilling to let him go.

"What happens now?"

His dad answered: "That's up to you, Jake."

PART FOUR: DOORWAYS

THIRTY

Would he wake up now? Or had the dream gone on for too long? Perhaps, even when he woke, there would be no way to tell, which reality had been dreamed by him, and which by someone else.

*   *   *

It is difficult for anyone, standing on the threshold of the fantastic, to resist curiosity and one's driving need for understanding, and not plunge its depths; to not explore the gaping maw of the cavern and the winding maze of tunnels unseen previously by human eyes; to not scour the darkness of the oceans and shed light on the blind beasts that lurk there; to not leave eternal footprints in the soft marshmallow sand, even walking the barren rock that is the Moon a thrill to the human spirit.

*   *   *

And Jake could feel the tug, a part of him that wanted to walk those dark fields, inhale the warm liquid air, and run his fingers through the thick wavering grass. But he needed to get his dad out of here; he needed his dad to be safe. Yet how often did you get a chance like this? If he turned his back now, he'd leave this opportunity behind him, and forever wonder what he had missed.

"Something's happening," his dad said.

And his dad was right: something churned in the darkness. Whatever oily blackness was in the sky also seemed to be on the horizon and there was something in it, thrashing at its borders, making the very darkness, at this distance, appear like a breathing cloud. He could hear a faint scuttling, like hundreds of marching feet, and he looked out over the hills to see if he could still make out where the Melting Man might have gone.

Before he knew he was going to do it, he'd stepped through the doorway, and now stood at the crest of a hill.

"Stop, Jake, don't...," his dad pleaded from the other side.

"Just for a minute," Jake said to his dad. "Wait here."

The first thing he noticed was that the grass wasn't really grass at all; it was too thick, like anemone tentacles, clutching to his sneakers and the cuffs of his pants, making each step a struggle. And the air was warmer than he'd imagined, sweat already soaking his shirt and beading on his forehead.

At the bottom of the hill, there was a deep indentation. He made his way down, to get a better look. He peered into the hole. It was dark and had a musty smell; it was crusty around the edges. Had this been one of those "amber pools" the Melting Man had talked about?

He stood and brushed the grit from his hands. He looked up and the darkness on the horizon was getting closer. There was something greasy about it, something that made him nervous. It didn't matter though; he'd be back with his dad before it reached him.

To his right, there was a small patch of odd-looking foliage. It reminded him of hanging vines wavering in the breeze, only hanging upwards from the ground, leafless stocks reaching towards the sky, ending in bloated clusters of pods. The vines seemed to reach for him as he drew closer.

Smell good...closer...yes...

They looked sticky, sprinkled with course, crystal sugar. He brought his hand out. He wanted to touch one of vines.

The closest stalk shot out and twisted about his wrist. It began to drag him towards the others. He pushed his heel into the ground and pulled back, trying to pull himself free.

The pods began to open, revealing wet, wriggling feelers.

Yes...smells good...smells so good...

The darkness was closing in. The sky was filled with it, seemed to push down on him. It felt as if it might collapse over him like a net.

"Run! Get out!"

Jake turned his head and saw the Melting Man running up the hill. The Melting Man's eyes sagged, his mouth torn open in a huge clown grimace.

Jake pulled against the vine, but it wouldn't let go; its feelers ran up his arm, leaving a sticky, snotty residue.

"Jake, come back." His dad's voice was faint; he shouldn't have wandered so far from the door.

The scuttling in the dark was growing louder and louder, alarmingly close to his current location.

With all his strength, he ripped himself free of the vine, the skin tearing on his arm.

No…closer…smells…

The Melting Man was still a ways off, running in a panic, and Jake saw that he was wounded, a gash torn across his chest that spilled creamy blood that fell and was absorbed hungrily by the anemone-grass. The thrashing darkness was closing in around him; it appeared as if something were knitting itself from the strands of shadow, working at a furious pace to form something material.

Jake turned away and ran towards where his dad stood in the doorway calling out to him. The anemones sucked at his feet, making his movements sluggish. He struggled forward.

"Go! Run!"

The scuttling in the dark filled his ears like the inconsistent sputter of water from a rusty faucet.

With some effort, he managed to tear his feet from the ground and flail up the hill and back to the standing doorway. He flopped forward so that his arms came through and his dad pulled him back up into the Melting Man's chamber.

He looked back and the Melting Man was running towards them, the darkness at his heels.

His dad was pulling him away from the door, down the hallway. "Come on, Jake. We have to get out of here."

"He's almost made it."

The Melting Man ripped through the doorway and collapsed. Jake could still see the terror coalescing from the dark.

The Melting Man stood, and his eyes met Jake's; he looked like an old and fragile man, jowls swinging. He took a step, hobbling towards where Jake stood.

His dad pulled at Jake's arm to keep him moving.

A flash of shadow cut the doorway like a whip and the Melting Man staggered to his knees.

Jake threw his dad's hands from him and ran down the hallway. He grabbed the limp and sagging Melting Man by the armpits and heaved. He could still see the field through the door. The anemone-grass jittered excitedly. The darkness had crossed the landscape and was beginning up the hill; the sound of thousands of eager clawed-feet was deafening.

Jake dragged the Melting Man as fast as he could. His dad rushed to help him and together they easily pulled the small emaciated creature along, who already seemed to be losing substance. They stopped at the end of the hallway.

The Melting Man was talking. His eyes were tiny now, no more than black marbles sunk into a wad of dough.

Jake glanced frantically at the doorway; the darkness was closing in.

"If this has all been a dream, never to age, never to sleep," the Melting Man gasped, "than perhaps, after all this time, I will finally awaken, in the light and in the warmth."

A deep rumble began in the lower register and rose up; the world began to tremble. Something had thrown itself at the door from the other side and was sucking at it, like a large mouth or tentacle, and was trying to force its way into the chamber.

"Close the door, Jake," his dad said.

"I don't know how."

Around them, the world was vibrating. The walls of excrement were coming down in sheets and clumps. Doorways were revealed, stacked against each other every few feet, each a different style and type, lining the hallway on both sides.

Jake looked down, and the Melting Man no longer had eyes. His body was soft, boneless—and dead. The sound the Melting Man's body made as it slumped to the ground was like settling oatmeal.

When Jake looked up, the door was closed, the trembling stopped.

He looked at his dad and his dad was smiling, unable to speak.

THIRTY-ONE

They wandered the hallways for a while — or they must have — examining the doors, hand in hand, as they might paintings in an art gallery, before crawling back up through their own doorway, down through the thin tunnel like a giant's nostril, and out into the sweet open air. They must have spent hours examining the doorways in a numbed curiosity, but later remembered little of what they'd seen, only fleeting threads of feeling that touched something obscured at the edge of the mind, then wafted away on a breeze gentle, but firm.

On the outside, before the strange and ancient tree, his dad produced the plain silver lighter from his pocket. Jake stared at it in his dad's palm. "Go on."

"But ZimZim's gone," Jake said.

"The fire never came from him."

"What if we left it?" But already he couldn't take his eyes from the glimmer of the lighter.

"For someone else to find? I don't think so."

Jake took the lighter. He looked at his dad, who nodded.

"I'll help you gather wood," his dad said.

*   *   *

They stood, side by side, hardly visible amongst the trees and the shadows. Night had fallen over them as they labored to collect and pile logs and sticks from the dried out drifts like giant nests of bone. Jake fondled the lighter in his sweaty palm.

The fire was massive. A true bonfire. A tribute to the forgotten. A blazing many-armed effigy, casting a glow over the countryside that must have been visible for miles, to all those with eyes and minds equipped to see it.

After a while, Jake and Harlan turned their backs on the pyre, and began the trudge home.

THIRTY-TWO

"You had that dream again, didn't you?"

"Yeah."

"The one you told me about? The one with the fire?"

"Yeah."

Harlan shook his head, gripping the steering wheel tight enough to turn his knuckles white. "I thought so," he said, "you're very pale this morning."

He watched his son — so small for his age — sitting in the passenger seat, staring out the window, watching the hotel fall behind them, as Harlan turned out of the parking lot.

"Can we go home today?" Jake asked.

Every morning, like a damn alarm clock; it was as if his son had forgotten they'd discussed this only yesterday. "I told you, Jake," he said. "We can't go back there. Not any time soon. We can't let them take me away from you."

He already knew what Jake was about to say: "But you didn't do it. It was…"

"ZimZim isn't real, Jake!"

Jake fell silent beside him, turning his eyes back to the window.

*　　*　　*

Sometime later, still hours before their next stop, he thought he saw a police car following them. It was the middle of the day and there was traffic and the clean white of the police car glared in the sun like a flashbulb hallucination, dodging in and out of view amongst the other cars. He tried to speed up, but the policeman kept pace, always just twenty or thirty yards behind. His heart beat a little too fast and his mouth was a little too dry; he began to sweat. He switched lanes and fell in behind a large camper, slowing down to let the policeman pass, but the policeman remained, always only a few yards behind. He kept imagining the police car getting closer, creeping up behind him, lights suddenly whirling; pulling him over to the side of the road.

What would he say? What would Jake say? Oh God, what would Jake say?

After a while, he looked in the rear-view mirror and the police car was gone. He didn't know how much time had passed, but his heart had slowed and he was starting to breathe more regularly again. Next to him, Jake continued to look out the window, listlessly; he sat there, not saying a word.

*   *   *

They crossed the countryside, like a faded and over-washed T-shirt, caught somewhere in this wasteland of yellow grasses and bleached sky; down South, he had family, a place to hide out for a while.

They stopped when Jake said he was hungry. He'd look for the pale glow of a McDonald's if he could—that had always been Jake's favorite—but his son ate without relish everything given him, not bothering with the toy, left discarded in the Happy Meal box at his feet.

Hours and miles crawled by; it seemed the sun would never set. The mountains on the horizon were like jagged and crumbling teeth against the dizzying immensity of the sky's open maw. Jake didn't say much, just drew in his notebook: strange things, creatures with large eyes and gangling limbs, smiling faces and frowning faces. His son had a very good imagination, but it was a little dark for his age. It made Harlan nervous. But someday his son was going to be a writer, or a movie director; he was going to tell stories, and that warmed his heart.

When the light finally began to fade from the sky, he took the nearest exit and drove slowly down what appeared to be the town's only road. He stopped at a small motel and slid in next to a truck in the parking lot, the only other vehicle there. He looked at Jake, who'd fallen asleep sitting up, so he left him in the car and staggered on numbed travel legs to the window that served as the motel's check-in counter. He paid for the room with cash and took the old brass key with him back to the car. Jake was still sleeping so he went around the side of the car, opened the door, and gently shook him. He blinked once and then his eyes were open and alert, glancing about nervously, instantly awake.

The room was musty, but serviceable; it reminded him of one particular summer in college, traveling from town to town with a small group of guys selling vacuum cleaners door to door. He'd taken the job to make a little extra money before classes started up again, and to get away from Jessica since they'd broken up and been fighting a lot at the time. All the guys had been young like him and they'd stayed in some pretty seedy places when they'd stop for the night, eager to hit the bars and get drunk and score with one of the local girls, which sometimes one of them even managed to do, filling the motel room with the sour organic smell of sex that they all had to share.

Jessica.

He stood in the motel room and watched Jake toss his backpack to the floor and slump onto the bed; Jake found the TV remote on the nightstand and the dull screen fuzzed into life. Had Jake started the house on fire? He must have. And Grace had died in his apartment and he knew how that must look to the authorities. They had to keep going. They had to get away. They were abandoning their old life: they didn't have a choice.

The TV buzzed. It was cold in the room and the heater under the window seemed only to blow a semi-warm musk; bitter cigarettes and stale sweat. After a while, they went to bed. Jake didn't seem to mind the room or the cold, but, when Harlan finally fell into a fitful surface sleep, despite the blankets heaped over him, he was still unable to control his trembling body.

* * *

By mid-morning of the next day the sun was a melting hole in the sky and the flat blacktop road, that split the feeble orange landscape like opposing tectonic plates, appeared to sway and bend—a mirage in the distant heat.

Harlan kept snatching glances at Jake. His dreams from last night were already fading—he rarely remembered them—but they made him uneasy; Jake made him uneasy. It felt as if a bundle of dark emotions were stalking him like a looming storm. He felt small in this unending desert, out in the open, as if a cruel pack of predators were toying with him and his son. All he could do was drive, on and on, but something wasn't right; the world had gone bad.

Jake had been in his dreams. Jake was running and running, and Harlan was chasing him. But that couldn't be right? He'd never hurt his son, his own flesh and blood; he was here to protect him. It was only a dream.

Jake was afraid of him.

"Hey, Dad?"

"Yes, Jake?"

"Can we go home today?"

* * *

He sat in the chair against the wall of the motel room smoking a cigarette and watching Jake, who sat on the bed flipping through the channels on the TV listlessly. His thoughts were a twisted ball of wires and him too numb to untangle them. He wanted a drink more than anything, but he wasn't drinking—for Jake's sake. Grief was never what you thought it was. He was sad, he supposed—upset a little—but too preoccupied with the stress of being on the run to process much else. Jake must feel the same way, he thought.

Slowly, he stood. He walked over to the bed to join Jake. He felt dull, a weight pressing down on him; inside him, his blood too thick, too much of a burden. He sat down next to his son.

"Jake?"

"Yeah, Dad?"

"Are you okay?"

"Sure, I guess."

"Is there anything I can do to make it better?"

Jake flipped the TV off angrily. "I just wanna go home."

Harlan put his arm around his son, who flinched, then relaxed. "I know, Jake. I'm sorry. It's all my fault. We'll be at grandpa's house soon; he'll take care of us, for a little while anyway."

"Grandpa's house?"

"You've never met him. Me and him, well, we had a bit of a falling out."

"I miss Mom."

Harlan took Jake fully in his arms. "I know, I know," he said. "I miss her too." He held his son tight, and comforted him as best he could.

*   *   *

He awoke slowly, shivering with cold. The TV spat silent static into the room. Careful not to waken Jake, who was fast asleep and snoring lightly in the crook of his arm, he reached for the remote and turned the TV off. He placed Jake down on the bed and pulled the covers up over them. He lay this way, trembling — his cold ankle and the rest of him slowly warming — for a while before he passed into a dreamless sleep.

The next day, they would reach Jake's grandfather's house.

THIRTY-THREE

Although the drive through the American Southwest took them only a couple of days, to Jake it felt like a journey across worlds; and yet, once they had gone so far, it felt as if it had taken place in only a single grand sun-bleached afternoon; an afternoon as obstinate and anesthetizing as a lifetime in the endless desert. The sandy grasses interspersed with yucca plants crawled by, nothing out of place, everything bland and normal; blank. Empty. He could remember very little of the journey, the meals, the nights in dark and musty motel rooms. He didn't think about much, tried purposefully to keep his mind from straying.

Driving South. Going South.

He wanted to know when they'd get wherever they were going. When could they go home? With ZimZim dead, his dreams had become oblique, swirling, incoherent nightmares. He missed his mom, couldn't really believe she was dead, and his dad had forgotten everything: he'd dismissed their experiences from his mind and would grow distant and weary if Jake tried to bring them up.

Mostly, he pushed back his tears and kept his eyes on the yellow and orange colors smearing by and the bluish mountains like absurd icebergs in the heat.

Going South. The hazy South.

Time crept back into his life about when the road turned from whistling blacktop to crunching dirt. As the wheels of the car encountered an increasing regularity of potholes and terrain in disrepair, he was jostled into the present. He turned his eyes out the window and the dust kicked up around them was a fog that trailed their progress.

"Almost there," his dad said.

His dad turned the car down another dirt road lined on either side by cattle fences made from rough wooden posts wrapped in barbed wire. Jake could even see a few cows, grazing distantly on the scraggly yellow grass.

A small farmhouse sat in the middle of the empty expanse, smaller than the rust-colored barn that lay a little ways behind it. The closer they became, the more rundown the house looked: it was really just a shack.

His dad pulled the car up in front of the house and killed the engine. They sat in the car, watching the dust settle over them, fogging the windshield in earth-colored grit. An elderly man came out of the house and stood on the porch, leaning against one of the wooden posts, watching them; waiting for them.

After a minute or two, his dad sighed. "Alright. Here we go. Come on, Jake. Meet your grandpa."

They got out of the car and stood in the dust.

The old man looked them up and down. "Well — you're late," he said.

"It took a little longer than I thought to get all the way out here," Harlan said.

"Uh-huh. Is this Jake?"

"Yeah. This is Jake."

Jake began to lift his hand, and then dropped it.

"Well, I suppose you ought to come on in." Jake's grandfather nodded his head for them to come up to the house.

"Thanks for having us," Harlan said. "We..."

"I don't wanna hear it," Jake's grandfather said, raising a weathered palm. "In trouble with the law are you? It doesn't matter. Nice to meet you, Jake."

The wooden steps up to the porch creaked as they walked up and followed the old man into the house.

*   *   *

They ate chicken and baked beans smothered in some sort of chili sauce, huddled around a small table with three different types of fold-out chairs. The beans were a little under-cooked and a little too spicy for Jake, but the chicken was moist and delicious. He ate until he was full and, almost immediately, felt his head grow drowsy, as if stuffed with cotton, too heavy for his neck to support any longer.

"He can have the bed in the back," he heard his grandfather's gravelly voice say.

And then his dad was leading him into a tiny

room and to the bed and he was asleep before his head sank into the plush comfort of the pillow.

*   *   *

He woke once during the night and it was dark out and his dad and his grandfather were still up and talking and he lay there listening until sleep overtook him once more.

"That's hard though, him losing his mom," his Grandfather's voice said.

"I'm just worried about him, you know? He's really shaken up by what happened — I can tell. I don't know what to do."

"Oh, don't worry about that. He's young still. He'll get over it."

"It's like he doesn't know me anymore. He thinks his imaginary friend did it all."

"Well, now, he'll get over that too. You just give him time."

"I've done horrible things. I've..." He could hear his dad crying.

A silent pause. Shifting in chairs. Creaking floorboards.

His grandfather spoke. "You can stay here as long as you need. No reason to worry. I'm not mad at you. You had to go and make your own way in the world, and now you'll have to lie in it. But you just do your lying here for a bit. It's been lonely out here since your mom died, anyway. I could use some help around here."

His dad said something then, began to talk about his secret past, but Jake couldn't stay awake, was gone from this conscious world.

*   *   *

Jake kicked at a clump of sagebrush, dislodging a worn-looking tumbleweed that immediately took off, rolling with the wind. It was hot and he was sweating and there wasn't much to do around here. He brought his hand up, shielding the sun from his eyes, and turned in a circle. It was flat, in every direction, for miles; it made him dizzy. The only plants that grew in the dusty ground were stunted shrubs and weeds and the occasional juniper tree.

Their water came up, from deep within the earth, through an ancient and calcified pump. His grandfather said it'd been put in by settlers close to three hundred years ago, and looking at it, he could almost believe it; it looked as if it could survive three hundred more, and probably would.

The electricity was spotty, causing the lights to flicker and sometimes go out for days so they were forced to live by candlelight, and his grandfather claimed to have never owned a TV. Was this what his dad had meant when he said, "Your grandfather lives like a goddamn hippie"?

His dad was standing at the crest of a small rise, looking off into the distance. "What are you doing?" Jake asked, walking up to stand next to his dad.

"Nothing. Just thinking."

"What about?"

His dad sighed. "About growing up out here—how lonely it was. I couldn't wait to leave. As soon as I was old enough…"

Jake kicked at the ground. He didn't know what to say.

EPILOGUE

His dad had told him once that dreams, like television, weren't real, and held no consequence in
the real world. And after months, and then years,
Jake could almost believe his dad was right, as his
dreams—and his grief—became less frequent, less
important, and less real. He supposed it was a part of
getting older, of growing up.

He looked back on his time at his grandfather's
farm fondly, always wishing he knew more about
the strange old man. But his grandfather didn't talk
much and his dad refused to discuss the subject in
more than vague generalities. On those occasions
when he'd pushed his dad for details, his dad had
fallen strangely silent and a grin had stretched his
face so large Jake had faltered and dropped the subject. That grin, like a gouging from a knife, brought
to mind strange and hazy memories of things he'd
rather not recall.

He had two dreams about his grandfather after his death. He couldn't remember the first one very well, but in it his grandfather was silently showing him around the old farm house, pointing first to the ancient water pump outside, and then pointing to a strange hatch inside the back of the house he'd never noticed before. In the second dream, he was in the open desert on a cold and moonless night, riding on horseback with his grandfather. Those similar though elusive dreams of the desert he'd had when he was younger finally began to make some sense to him. He'd dreamed of them. He'd dreamed of *this*. In this version, his mother rode up to them and smiled at Jake. She was radiant. They all waited for his dad, but after a while his grandfather said, "Don't worry, he'll be along soon enough," and they rode on. The hooves of the horses kicked up dust, and the snorts and huffs from the beasts formed ghostly clouds in the crisp cool air. They rode together through the night, parting the darkness like a veil, and there were things in the darkness, things that scuttled and ran alongside them, always just out of sight, but his grandfather held a great torch of fire aloft before them, forcing the darkness back. And in the dream he knew his dad was safe because his dad also had a torch and he was somewhere up ahead in all that darkness and all that cold, and he knew that whenever he got there his dad would pass the fire to him. Maybe, he thought in the dream, his parents understood more than they'd ever let on.

When he eventually returned to his grandfather's house years later, it sat lonely and beaten in the crackling sun, more like an old mining compound than a farm. Even the *For Sale* sign looked ancient and worn, sticking up at a canted angle amongst a pile of rocks. It was a windy day and sheets of dust cast a grimy veil over the landscape, muting colors and whistling hopelessly. Squinting, Jake stepped from his car. The water pump remained by the side of the house, as it would forever, reminding the bleak surface of this land that there were still riches and mysteries buried beneath that which could be seen. Gritting his teeth, he pushed himself up those wooden steps and into the house.

The house was just as his grandfather had left it — the table, chairs, mismatched dishes and tin cups still in the cupboards in the kitchen; the tiny bed in the back bedroom where he'd slept all those exhausted nights. On impulse, he pulled the silver lighter from his jacket pocket and looked at it in his palm. He didn't know why he'd brought it, didn't even know why he'd kept it all this time. Still, it felt good to hold in his hand, natural. And then he discovered the hatch in the floor. He'd never noticed it before, there at the back of the house, as if he'd been meant to discover only just then, in this way and at that time.

Wake up, Jake…

He crouched before it, vaguely remembering a hallway of doors and the wondrous things that could be stumbled upon once one ventured through them.

I am awake…

He realized then that as he'd grown older and matured into adulthood, he'd forgotten many things. As a grown man he'd lived a quiet life, an ordinary life, but now he could feel the ordinary evaporating, the darkness and cold falling away like an old overcoat slipping free of him. The air shimmered with barely repressed energy.

Clutching the lighter tight, he closed his eyes then opened the hatch.

His new life was about to begin.

ABOUT THE AUTHOR

Keith Deininger is an award winning writer and poet. His short fiction can be found in numerous publications in the United States and in the UK. He grew up in the American Southwest and currently resides in Albuquerque, New Mexico with his wife and their three dogs. *The New Flesh* is his first novel. Visit him at: www.KeithDeininger.com.

CPSIA information can be obtained at www.ICGtesting.com
Printed in the USA
BVOW05s0926200314

348259BV00008B/155/P